JOSHUA'S CHOICE

SEVEN AMISH BACHELORS BOOK 3 (AMISH ROMANCE)

SAMANTHA PRICE

PRINT ISBN 978-1976371868

CHAPTER 1

JOSHUA FULLER, the third son of Obadiah and Ivy Fuller, knew many girls liked him. He often noticed the girls at community events and meetings huddled in groups whispering about him and sneaking glances his way. He'd taken many girls out on buggy rides, but had never taken the same girl twice. Lately, though, he hadn't asked any girls out and there was but one reason for that.

His gaze swept around the crowd, and as usual, his eyes settled on that one reason, that one girl. Her name was Adeline Miller. She wasn't the prettiest in the group, but neither was she the plainest. There was something about her quiet and gentle nature that had reached out and taken hold of his heart. A few minutes ago, she had become his new sister-in-law since his older brother had just married Adeline's older sister, Lucy.

His mother didn't like Adeline's family, but Levi had unknowingly paved the way for him to marry Adeline when he married Lucy. At seventeen years of age, Adeline was a little young to be married, but if she agreed and both sets of parents agreed too, there wouldn't be a problem.

He looked over at Lucy and Levi chatting happily at the wedding breakfast table and then saw the parents of the bride and groom at a nearby table. The fathers were talking comfortably and eating away at the delicious foods. The mothers looked a bit stiff, but they were chatting politely with one another—that was a positive sign and better than them ignoring one another as they would've done at one time. They weren't friends, but maybe one day they could be. Shared *grosskinner* had a way of softening hard hearts.

He looked back at Adeline, hoping no young men had noticed her. He smiled when he saw she was still surrounded by girls. He loved her name too, Adeline. He could imagine them walking in the woods, and her playfully running away and then hiding behind a tree, and he would whisper her name in the wind. *Adeline. Adeline, where are you?* Then, a few moments later, she would tap him on the shoulder and cause him to jump. A soft chuckle escaped Joshua's lips over his heart-warming daydreams.

"What are you laughing at?" a deep male voice inquired.

Joshua swung around to see his next-in-line younger brother, Jacob. "Nothing."

"It must be something. A serious young man like you doesn't laugh at nothing."

Joshua gave him a playful shove. "Get out of here. Who are you calling a serious young man?"

Jacob grinned widely. "Well that's what you are, aren't you?"

"About as serious as you."

Jacob looked over at the girls. "Maybe you were smiling at that group of people over there."

"Nee!" Joshua snapped.

Jacob wasn't easily fooled. "Is that right?"

Joshua frowned at him.

Jacob continued to stare at the girls. "Let me guess... Which one of them takes your fancy?"

"None of them do," Joshua said, hoping his brother wouldn't notice his treasured Adeline.

"There's Mary Lou, but you wouldn't like her because she used to date Isaac, so she's out. You said before you'd never date her, I remember that. Then there are some girls who are too young for you... But wait, then there's Nella."

"Cut it out, and stop being rude." Nella had made no secret about liking Joshua and Jacob would've known that.

3

"Nella is quite attractive. I can see the two of you getting hitched. I reckon we'll be at Nella's folks' in about four months and you'll be pledging your lifelong love to her."

Joshua shook his head. "You've got it wrong."

"Have I?" His lips twitched. "Hmm, then. Let's see. What about Becky?"

He looked over at Becky. She was often standing by herself and didn't have many friends. "Wrong again. Although there's nothing wrong with Becky."

"Who said there was anything wrong with her?"

"Not me," Joshua said.

"Me either. And it would be convenient since her brother and Timothy are best friends."

"I've got a good idea," Joshua said.

"What's that?" Jacob asked.

"Why don't you go harass somebody else?"

One side of Jacob's lips lifted into a crooked smile. "I've already done that and now it's your turn."

Joshua rolled his eyes and then shook his head. "I can believe that." Joshua looked back at Lucy and Levi, and then rubbed his neck. "It seems funny that two of our *brieder* are now married."

"There's nothing funny about it."

"You want to get married someday, don't you?" Joshua asked Jacob.

"Maybe, and maybe not."

Joshua stepped back in shock. That was not the

answer he was expecting. "Don't you want to have a family someday?"

"Maybe and maybe not," Jacob repeated smugly.

"Why do you have to joke all the time? Why can't you just give a straight answer?"

"Because I don't know at this stage. Okay, I'll be serious. If you must know, I'm trying to find a woman who's the right fit for me. I can't think of anything worse than making the wrong choice and being stuck for fifty years with a shrew or someone who bores me to tears. And what if I like someone and that only lasts a few years and then turns sour?" He shook his head. "The whole idea of marriage scares me." Jacob stared at his older brother. "There. Is that serious enough for you?"

Joshua smiled, thinking his brother was joking again, but then he saw from his face that Jacob was serious. "You're really scared?"

"And you should be too. You can be attracted to a girl because she's pretty, but have you noticed how women—some of these women right here in the community have doubled and tripled their size after only a year or two of marriage?"

"That's probably only after they've had children. If a woman's given you a child you can't complain about her figure. Anyway, you don't just marry a woman because of her looks." Joshua was trying to make Jacob see sense. He knew his brother was seen as handsome because he was popular with the girls, but he didn't have to be so vain about it. Jacob's problem might be that he seemed to be trying to find a woman who was as good looking as he. Not only that, he seemed to require some guarantee she'd stay that way. "And have you ever looked in the mirror lately? You're not exactly a prize yourself."

Jacob gave him a shove. "I reckon I'm all right. All the girls seem to think so, too. I could walk up to any one of them, ask them out, and there won't be one of them says, 'No.'"

Joshua scoffed. "I doubt it."

"Okay, see that group of girls over there? I'll ask each one of them out over the next two weeks and if one of them says no, I'll do all your chores for a whole year."

Joshua looked over the group his brother was referring to. Adeline was in that group. Joshua jumped in front of him blocking his view. "No don't!"

Jacob took a step to the side and studied the girls once more. "Why not?"

"All right you win. I like one of the girls. There, satisfied?"

"Not entirely. You're still holding out on me. Which one is she?"

"I'm joking! I just don't think it's a good idea. It's stupid." Joshua spoke with all the authority he could, using his best older-brother voice.

Jacob carefully studied his face. "I think you do like one of them, going by your worried face and flushed cheeks." Jacob then pointed his finger at Joshua's lips. "And your trembling bottom lip."

Joshua swiped at his brother's hand and Jacob pulled it out of his way just in time. "Cut it out! I don't have a trembling anything."

Jacob stepped past his brother and closer to the girls. "Let me see which one I think you'd fancy."

"Don't you have anything better to do with your time?"

"We're at a wedding, what else is there to do other than socialize?" Jacob breathed in, fixed a smile on his face, and started walking toward the group of girls.

Joshua quickly put his foot out and tripped him up. Jacob nearly fell over but managed to catch his footing.

He narrowed his eyes at Joshua. "What was that for?"

Joshua shook his head. "I told you not to."

"Look, we settled this years ago. You're not the boss of me."

"Hmm. I remember that day and as I recall we settled that I *am* the boss of you."

Jacob huffed. "Just give me her name and I'll strike her off my list. I won't compete with you. Whoever she is, you can have her."

"Really?"

"Yeah, there's none here that appeals to me enough to choose one, so I'm willing to keep away."

"*Denke,* Jacob."

Jacob laughed. "You've got it bad."

"It's Adeline, and if you so much as talk to her, or tell anyone I like her, you'll live to regret it."

Jacob raised his eyebrows. "Adeline, Lucy's younger sister, Adeline Miller?"

"*Jah*, that's the one. There's only one Adeline."

Jacob looked over at her, then turned back to Joshua and put a hand on his shoulder. "There's no need to rob the cradle. There's plenty of girls your own age to choose from."

"She's seventeen."

Jacob looked over at Adeline. "I reckon she's only fifteen if she's a day."

"I overheard Lucy telling someone she's seventeen."

"What is it about her that has you so worked up?"

What could Joshua say? He thought she was delightful. Every time she smiled, her eyes sparkled. When she giggled it was like the sweet music of a thousand angels singing. She walked—no glided—with the grace of a swan moving along a still and tranquil lake. There was no way he could tell his brother any of that. "She appeals to me."

"I figured that, but why?"

Joshua looked over at Adeline once more. She was a sweet flower who stood out above all the others, but he wouldn't expect his arrogant and conceited brother to understand the subtleties of anything to do with love. Joshua hoped that Adeline might one day return those feelings. And he was yet to know how to approach her; that's why he was holding back and observing her from afar. He couldn't just ask her on a buggy ride because he'd risk her saying no. He had to get closer to her and hope she would fall in love with him.

"I said, 'Why?'" Jacob repeated.

Joshua turned back to see a stupid lop-sided grin on Jacob's face. "I can't say, I just find her appealing."

"Each to his own, I suppose," Jacob said.

"You would've dated all the single girls in the community about now, wouldn't you?" Joshua asked.

"*Jah*, I'll have to go visiting soon and see what talent's in the other communities."

Joshua shook his head. "You're just ridiculous. What will *Mamm* say if you choose a girl in some far-flung community? You know what she's like about not having any girls and wanting us to marry so she can have someone who's like a *dochder* to her."

Jacob looked over at Lucy and Levi, and then moved closer to Joshua and whispered, "We both know *Mamm* wasn't overjoyed when Isaac married Hazel and she wasn't happy about Lucy either. I don't see her jumping for joy if you and Adeline get together."

Jacob wasn't telling Joshua something he didn't already know. He was well aware his mother wasn't happy with their two oldest brothers' choices in wives, but as much as he loved his mother, no one was going to have a say in who his wife was going to be. "We're talking about you, not me."

"I'm just looking out for you. If I don't, who will?" Jacob asked.

Joshua frowned. "I'm old enough to look out for myself. I'm just trying to protect you from our *mudder*. If you look in another community, you're going to find a woman there. If you stay here, you'll eventually come across someone suitable; I'm sure of it."

"The point I was trying to make was she mightn't like it, but I can't live my life around what the woman does and doesn't like. I'm a grown man. If I fall in love with a girl from another community *Mamm* will just have to accept that."

"So, you *are* looking for that one special love?"

"I'm looking for it, but I don't expect to find it. I'm looking for love … I need to find a girl I'm so in love with that if she ends up eating herself stupid and looking like a fat old cow after we marry, I won't care."

Joshua shook his head in disgust. "I'm sure *Gott* has something good in store for you, Jacob."

"What do you mean by that?"

"Maybe you need to be taught a lesson. You talk about women like they're not people. They are tender-hearted beings that we must protect and look after."

Jacob's face soured. "You've gone soft. You must be truly in love."

"Don't make a joke of everything, Jacob. Love is a serious thing and choosing a *fraa* is too. She will become part of you, and you will become part of her. The two of you shall become one in *Gott's* sight."

Jacob roared with laughter and slapped Joshua on the back. "It sounds like you've been to too many weddings."

"I'm hoping the next one will be mine."

Jacob gave a gruff sound from the back of his throat. "I'm off to find the most attractive girl that I can drive home tonight, and trust me, she won't say no to this face." Jacob gave Joshua a wink.

Joshua couldn't believe his brother's arrogant words and he hoped he'd learn his lesson sooner rather than later. Jacob was a good-looking man, but with his awareness of those looks, pride had crept into his heart.

Pushing his brother's words out of his mind, Joshua looked back at Adeline. She caught his eye, and then quickly looked away. He was sure he saw a gentle blush color her cheeks before she turned aside. What would he do if Adeline rejected him? He wouldn't be able to bear it. He had to figure out a way for her to get to know him in a slow and natural way. It had to help that her sister had just married his brother.

CHAPTER 2

ADELINE TURNED AWAY as quick as she could when she saw Joshua Fuller staring at her—again. The only thing she could do was turn her back because she didn't want him to see her beet-red cheeks that were burning.

Her younger sister, Catherine, and she were wedding attendants for their oldest sister, Lucy's wedding. It was exciting to have the first wedding in the family and Catherine and she had spent the last few weeks helping Lucy sew all the wedding dresses and the suits for Levi and his two friends.

As Adeline had sewed, she'd imagined what it would be like when her wedding day came. Who would she marry? Now the only man she had on her mind was Joshua. She hadn't given him any thought until she noticed him during the wedding preparations, and he'd come to her attention because he kept looking at her.

Little by little, he began to grow on her. Adeline wondered what Joshua saw in her, and whether he would rule her out as a potential wife for being too young. Or did he plan to wait until she was older before he made a move? She was ready to get married right now. That was what she wanted and then she'd be a young *mudder* and grow with her *kinner*. She considered she was equally as mature as Lucy. Adeline had always felt older than her years.

"There he is," she heard one of the girls whisper to another of the girls in her group.

She looked over to see that it was Mary Lou speaking. Quickly, Mary Lou fixed a smile on her face and start walking. In Adeline's heart, she knew she was heading to talk to Joshua. Upset by the thought of the more experienced woman talking to the man she liked, Adeline walked away. When she'd taken a few steps, she turned around to find out she'd been right.

As Mary Lou talked with Joshua, Adeline studied Joshua's face to see if she could find some hint of whether he liked Mary Lou. She knew from her older sister that Mary Lou liked Joshua and she'd been asking about him. There must've been something about the Fuller boys that Mary Lou liked, given her history with them. All of them were handsome, that was for certain. Mary Lou was older than Joshua, but from the way she was talking with him, it didn't bother her in the slightest.

The other person who stood in the way of Adeline and Joshua's happiness was Nella. Nella had asked Lucy for help in pairing her with Joshua. It seemed everybody wanted to marry Joshua.

Adeline heaved a sigh and walked over to sit next to her newly married sister, sitting happily at the wedding table with her new husband.

Lucy left off talking to Levi and smiled at her younger sister.

"Are you having a good time?" Adeline asked her.

"I am. Are you?"

"Jah. Everyone is."

Lucy sighed. "It was a beautiful wedding if I do say so."

"It hasn't finished yet," Adeline said.

"I know and I'm going to enjoy every minute of it. You don't have to sit by me. Go talk to friends, or make some new ones." Lucy leaned closer to her. "There are lots of visitors. You might even find a boy that you like."

She kept it secret from her sister that she'd already found one. If Lucy found out, she might mention something to Levi, and then Levi would surely say something to Joshua. That would be so embarrassing.

And what if she was wrong about him liking her? There was always that chance. What if Joshua had been looking at her for an entirely different reason? It was possible he was looking at her because he thought she was odd, or maybe he just wanted to be friends with his new sister-in-law. Adeline then noticed Nella beckoning for her to come back.

"I'll be back in a minute," Adeline said to Lucy.

"Take your time—mingle."

Adeline hurried over to see what Nella wanted. "What's wrong?"

"You guessed it. Something's very wrong."

"I can tell by your face. What is it?"

"It's that Mary Lou. She's been talking to Joshua for the longest time."

Adeline looked down at the ground. The last person she wanted to talk to Nella about was Joshua. It was awkward having two of her friends liking Joshua.

"Will you go over and join the conversation? It'll look too obvious if I do it," Nella said.

"I can't."

"Of course you can. Just go up and talk about something with them."

Adeline shook her head. *"Nee,* I can't do it. I'm too shy to do that."

"Well, at least go close enough to hear what they're saying."

"Why don't you?"

Nella's eyes opened wide. "Because he probably already knows I like him and it'll be too obvious. It'll look like I'm jealous and that I'm a different type of girl from the one I am."

"But what will he think of me if I go and barge into their conversation?" Adeline bit her lip. She wanted Joshua to have a good impression of her.

"You don't like him, so it doesn't matter."

Adeline nodded. She had to let Nella think that.

"If you don't do that for me, I don't know who will." Nella stood there looking around. "I can't see anyone else I can ask. There's no one I can trust like I trust you."

It was unfortunate that Nella kept saying things like that, not realizing Adeline's feelings. It caused pangs of guilt to shoot through Adeline's body. "There's not much you can do if he likes Mary Lou. He'll just choose whoever he likes best."

"Nee, that can't happen." Nella put a hand on her heart. "I couldn't take that. I simply will die if I don't marry him."

"You surely can't mean that. He's just a man."

"He might be just a man to you, but he's the *only* man to me. The only man I want to marry. I can't stop thinking about him and I've felt this way for the longest time."

"And you think he knows you like him?"

"I think so. I've dropped enough hints around his friends and *brieder,* so he'll be brave enough to ask me out."

"Brave enough?"

Nella nodded. "You've got a lot to learn before you

17

start dating, Adeline. Men get nervous too. It's not just girls who get nervous."

Nella was older than Adeline, as were most of Adeline's friends. "I didn't know. I mean, I didn't realize they got nervous as well."

"I'll have to take you under my wing and teach you a few things since Lucy will be busy setting up a new home and having *bopplis*. She'll have no time for you anymore."

Adeline whipped her head around to look back over at Lucy. They had been so close and now she felt like she was losing her sister, and she didn't like it. It was nice to have an older sister to learn from and also a younger one to teach. Being the middle child, Adeline felt she had the best of both worlds, but now she'd only have Catherine to teach. *"Denke* for your offer, Nella. I guess she will be too busy for me."

"I'll be glad to teach you what I know."

They both looked back at Mary Lou and Joshua, still talking.

"I don't like it. They look like they're getting along far too well."

"I don't see that there's anything we can do about it." Adeline bit her lip.

"I do. I'm going to grab a plate of food and carry it around. I'll offer them something." Nella pulled on Adeline's sleeve. "You do it too, so it won't look odd that I'm the only one."

"I told you I don't want to go near them, or anywhere near them."

"*Nee*, you won't have to. I'll do this side of the crowd and you do the other."

Adeline gave in. "Okay, I can do that."

"Let's go."

WHILE JOSHUA WAS PASSING the time talking to Mary Lou, he managed to keep an eye on Adeline. He saw her taking a platter of food around to people. That was just the sweetest, kindest thing that he'd seen anyone do at a wedding. It confirmed to him that she was the right woman for him. He must've been staring at her for too long because Mary Lou had noticed that something else had taken his attention.

"What is it?" She looked to where he'd been gazing.

"Nothing," he answered.

"If you're hungry I can get you something."

"I've had quite enough, *denke.*"

"Anyway, why don't you and I do something sometime?" Mary Lou startled him with her boldness.

"I'd consider it, but I've got quite a bit going on these next few weeks. My calendar is jammed and things will be worse with Levi away for the next week or so."

"Me too." She giggled. "I'm busy too. I didn't mean

now, I meant when Lucy and Levi come back from their visiting."

"We'll see," he said, feeling it would be too cruel to give an outright 'no.' When he saw Mary Lou's disappointed face, he felt sorry for her. She had very nearly become his sister-in-law, so she was more than just a friend. "When they come back, a few of us could do something together as a group."

Her face lit up. "You mean it?"

"Why not?"

"I can hardly wait. What will we do?"

He shrugged his shoulders. "I've got no idea. Why don't we wait until Levi comes back and I'll arrange something then?" She looked so pleased and excited he was tempted to point out that it wasn't a date, but again, he didn't want to be cruel. Going on a group outing was just that, a group outing. "I'll ask some of the others when the time comes."

"Okay."

They were interrupted by Nella offering them chocolate shoo fly pies.

He took a shoo fly pie off the plate. "*Denke,* Nella."

She flashed him a smile and then said to Mary Lou, "Would you like one too?"

"*Nee, denke.* I'm watching my figure." She fluttered her eyelashes and looked at Joshua from underneath them.

"I never have to worry about mine," Nella said. "I eat as much as I want and never gain weight."

Not to be outdone, Mary Lou replied, "Many people are like that when they're young and it catches up with them when they're older."

Nella pouted at Mary Lou.

"When it comes to good food and shoo fly pies, I'm afraid I don't give a thought to my figure," Joshua said, which made the two girls go into fits of giggles. While they were twittering, he looked around for Adeline and saw her offering food to a group of young men. He didn't like it. He had to be quick and put together a plan to win her heart and her hand.

"What were the two of you talking about before I came up?" Nella asked.

"Joshua was talking about something we're going to do together later."

When Nella looked shocked, Joshua didn't want it to get around that he was going on a date with Mary Lou, because that's how Mary Lou had made it sound. *"Jah, we're going on a group outing with some other people and you're very welcome to join us. I suggested to Mary Lou that when Lucy and Levi come back from visiting, we'd go out and do something together as a group."*

"All the young people?" Nella asked.

Joshua nodded. *"Jah."*

"I'd love to."

"Good." Joshua felt sorry for Nella when he saw Mary Lou glaring at her. She wasn't happy at all. "If you two would excuse me, that shoo fly pie has made me hungry for some cheesecake."

He hurried away leaving the two girls glaring at each other.

CHAPTER 3

"MIND IF I HAVE ONE?"

Adeline turned around and looked up into the face of Joshua Fuller. It was the first time she'd seen him so close. Her heart leaped as though she was seeing him for the first time. His eyes were a dark green hazel, almost brown, and his skin was tanned yet smooth and creamy. She knew his skin would be soft to the touch. His lips offered a gentle smile that widened the longer she took to answer his question. "Oh, one of these?" She lifted up the plate of mini cheesecakes.

"*Jah.*" He chuckled softly. "One of those."

"Of course." He took one and held it in his hand. "A group of us are going to go out together and do something exciting." He gave a little chuckle. "It will be when your *schweschder* and Levi come back from visiting."

"What are you going to do?"

"I'm not sure, is there something you'd like to do?"

"I'm invited?"

"Of course you are. I should've asked you. I meant to. Would you like to come with us?"

"Oh." Her cheeks burned and she wished she knew how to act and what to say. She didn't have much experience with the opposite sex. If only she'd had an older brother, then she would've had young men coming to the house and she would've gotten used to them. "I guess I'll come then."

"Good, I'll check back with you closer to the time."

No longer could she look into his eyes. With her stomach aflutter, all she could do was to give a quick nod, and then she hurried away.

ADELINE PUT the plate of food back onto the table and ran to Nella, and stopped when she saw Nella deep in conversation with Mary Lou. She stayed back, just close enough to hear what was being said.

"He asked me out on a date and then you came up and pushed your way into everything." Mary Lou was angry going by the tone of her voice and the way she was glaring at Nella.

"It wasn't a date, he said it was a group outing for all the young people."

Adeline was heartbroken. It sounded like Joshua had given the same invitation to Mary Lou and Nella that he'd just given to her. Then it dawned on Adeline that he had said right away that it was a group thing. Somehow, she'd chosen to ignore that part of the invitation. Apparently, so had Mary Lou. Again, she focused in on what the girls were saying.

"It probably wasn't a group outing until you pushed yourself in," Mary Lou replied.

"Stop it, Mary Lou. You're being mean."

"I'm not. I'm just telling you how it is. He's nice and didn't want to make a fool of you, so he had to invite you too because you overheard him. That's what kind of a man he is. But it's really me he's interested in."

"It's not; it's me."

Fearing she'd be drawn into the conflict between the two young women, Adeline turned on her heel and went to walk away, but Nella saw her.

"Adeline, come here."

Adeline turned around and slowly walked over. *"Jah?"*

"Who do you think Joshua Fuller likes, Mary Lou or me?"

She could feel Mary Lou glaring at her while she thought how best to answer that question. "How would I know? I wouldn't have any idea."

"She's just a child," Mary Lou said.

Nella frowned at Mary Lou. *"Jah,* let's talk about age. Exactly how old are you, Mary Lou? You're a lot older than Joshua."

"Age doesn't matter."

"You're far too old for Joshua, and you threw yourself at Levi and you were too old for him, too. You should go for a man your own age."

"I don't think there should be ugly talk like this," Adeline said. "Joshua will choose the woman he wants. There's no need for us to argue amongst ourselves. *Gott* has somebody for each of us."

Mary Lou scowled at Adeline, took three strides to stand right next to her, and leaned over so her lips were close to Adeline's ear. "You have no idea what you're saying. You're too immature." Then Mary Lou shot Nella a filthy look before she stomped away from both of them.

Nella took a deep long breath. "I shouldn't have gotten into an argument like that. It was pointless. She just makes me so mad, though. I don't know why she does, she just does. It's almost like she tries to set me off. I really hope she doesn't marry Joshua, or I'll simply die."

"Nella, you must stop saying you'll die. It's not a good thing to say."

"I only just said it then. I don't say it all the time."

"You do. You've said that at least four or five times

today. You'll die if Joshua does this, you'll die if Joshua does that. You'll die if you don't marry him. Die, die, die."

Nella giggled. "Okay, I'll stop saying it. *Denke,* Adeline, I didn't realize. I'll have to listen to what I say."

CHAPTER 4

"Why were you talking to Joshua? Do you like him?"

"He's one of our *bruders*-in-law now." Adeline didn't want Catherine to know she liked Joshua in case her younger sister let it slip to someone.

"Mine too, but he didn't look for me and talk to me. I watch people and study them. He likes you."

"Nee, he doesn't."

"And perhaps—"

"I don't!"

"Don't what?" A slight smile turned Catherine's lips upward.

"Whatever you were just about to say."

Catherine giggled. "You like him. I'm telling *Mamm* you like him."

It was no use. Her sister knew her too well. "If you

tell *Mamm* anything I'll tell her how you broke her wedding clock."

Catherine's eyes opened wide. It was a secret they'd both held for many years. "You wouldn't!"

"I would."

"I'm right anyway about your liking Joshua Fuller. That's kinda weird with him being your *bruder*-in-law," Catherine said smugly.

"I don't want to talk about it."

"If you like him you should tell me because Nella likes him too."

"Nella's *your* friend," Adeline said. It was Catherine who had first become good friends with Nella despite their age difference.

"And yours."

"All right, I like him, so do you see my problem? If it's *Gott's* will that something happens between us then something will. I don't believe in chasing a man. If he likes me, things will happen in their own time." Adeline hoped she'd said enough to keep Catherine quiet.

Catherine looked in Joshua's direction. "It's okay. I won't tell anyone anything."

"*Gut, denke.*"

She fixed her eyes back onto Adeline. "Just don't tell *Mamm* about the clock. She'll be so upset."

"Okay, I won't."

WHEN THE BELL rang for lunch at his father's large joinery company, Joshua stopped work. He and his six brothers, his father, and his sister-in-law, Hazel, all worked in the company. Levi had moved on to take over the quoting for jobs along with the eldest brother, Isaac, but Joshua was happier to stay in the shop, working directly with the wood. Joshua wasn't good at talking to people and making sales like his older brothers, but he loved everything about wood—the grain, the smell of a freshly sawn piece of timber, and the way a raw piece could be fashioned into something beautiful, yet useable. Each piece of timber had its own peculiarities much like every person has their own personality.

Every day at lunchtime, he and his brothers would walk up the road to have lunch at the same café. As they were walking past Hazel's office, Hazel called out to Joshua.

He stuck his head through her doorway. *"Jah,* Hazel?"

"I have a surprise for you."

"For me?"

"Jah. Come with me."

Joshua followed Hazel through the back of the storage area, opened the back door, and there was Mary Lou. He stared at her, wondering what she was doing and why she was standing there grinning. Then his gaze fell to the table she was standing beside. It was a small round table covered with food, and nearby were two chairs.

He looked at Mary Lou, and then looked back at Hazel, waiting for some kind of explanation.

"Surprise, Joshua!" Mary Lou said. "I've made lunch for you."

CHAPTER 5

JOSHUA'S HEART SANK. This was the worst possible thing that could've ever happened to him. Now he knew for sure that Mary Lou was pursuing him. He couldn't understand it. He had given her absolutely no hint that he liked her back, and he remembered how she had thrown herself at Levi after their oldest brother had rejected her. He felt sorry for her and thought she was a nice enough girl, but he definitely didn't want to have lunch with her.

"What's all this?" He looked over the table of food while wondering how best to handle the situation.

"I made a special lunch just for you."

"That's very kind of you, but it's not even my birthday."

She giggled. "I figured you needed to be spoiled. Everyone needs that once in a while. Sit down."

He turned around hoping to get help from Hazel, but she'd disappeared completely. He tugged at the neck of his shirt to loosen it. He felt he was being strangled. "It's very kind of you."

"That's just the kind of person I am—kind." She giggled again. "Sit down," she ordered.

He pulled one chair away from the other one, so he wouldn't be sitting too close. There was no other way around it, by the end of the lunch he had to let her know he didn't return her feelings—even if he had to tell her outright.

"I've got cold roast chicken, coleslaw—"

"It all looks delicious."

"I'm a very good cook. I'm not being prideful, I'm just saying the truth."

"Mm. I can see that." He went to take a plate and she quickly snatched it from him and started filling it with food.

"I'll do that. I don't want you to lift a finger."

"Denke."

"How has your day been so far?

"Very busy. It's usually hectic around here. Aren't you working today?"

"Nee. I've got the day off."

"That was very kind of you to make all this, and now you've wasted your day off on me."

"It's not wasted. I wanted to do this. Wasn't it a nice surprise?"

"A huge surprise." He scratched his forehead. "Why do all this for me, though?"

She looked across at him just as she was piling chicken on his plate. "You work so hard, you deserve a good meal."

"That's enough chicken, *denke*." He took the plate from her and placed it in front of him. "The boys and I usually go up the road to the coffee shop for lunch."

"I know, I saw you all there once. You probably don't remember."

He didn't.

"Eat. Don't wait for me," she said.

He cut a piece of chicken and then glanced over at her to see that she was looking pleased with herself. It was a lovely gesture she'd made. "You put a lot of effort into this. I appreciate it." He popped the chicken into his mouth.

She fluttered her lashes at him. "You're worth it."

He nearly choked as he swallowed.

"Have some water." She passed him a glass. "Or, maybe I should've got wine."

"Definitely not wine. Not while I'm working."

"*Ach, jah.* That's right, but since you work for your *vadder*, maybe you could take the rest of the day off so we can do something?"

He shook his head. It was a dreadful idea, and her perception was all wrong. The fact that he worked for his family meant he had to work harder to prove himself, not take time off whenever he felt like it. "It's because I work for my *vadder* that I can't. I'm the main one in the workshop now that Levi is doing the quotes and ordering with Isaac."

"What do you have to order? Don't you make all the kitchens here?"

"*Jah,* we do, but there's hinges and handles and so forth, we don't make them. Then some of them are bits and pieces, and, for the more unusual work, we make all the special orders. Most everything we do is custom made." He knew he probably wasn't making much sense, but he'd never been good with words. That's one of the reasons he didn't deal directly with the customers.

"Well, surely there wouldn't be many of those and wouldn't you already have a stock of hinges and handles?"

He nodded. "Some." He kept eating, hoping she wouldn't ask again for him to take the day off. How would he let her down gently? He didn't want to hurt her feelings especially when she'd gone out on a limb to do this. It was the most awkward he'd felt in his life.

"Are you enjoying the food?"

"It's *wunderbaar.* Much better than the food from the café."

"We'll have to do this again."

He couldn't let it go on without saying something. He swallowed hard. "Look, Mary Lou, I'm very flattered that you've done all this just for me. The thing is, you deserve someone much better than a simple man like me."

"Don't be silly, Joshua. You're the most wonderful man I've ever met."

How could what she said be true when she'd also liked his two older brothers? He stared at her, hoping he could put the right words together to honestly convey his feelings while at the same time sparing hers. "There is a significant age difference between us."

"Oh, Joshua. That's so sweet." She fluttered her long eyelashes at him once more. "I don't mind that you're younger."

Joshua looked down at his water, now wishing it was wine. He could do with a stronger drink right now. The girl just wasn't taking a hint. He tried again. "We don't have anything in common."

"We are both ... in the same community."

"And?" he asked.

Now she looked hurt. "I don't know what you mean."

He didn't either; he was clutching at straws.

Then a smile broke out on her face. "It doesn't matter. Men and women don't have to have anything in common. I know what the problem is, you've never had a girlfriend, have you?"

"It's true, I haven't. Nothing serious anyway."

Her face beamed. "That's why you don't know how things work."

He shook his head. "I'm pretty sure I do know how things work."

"You're not eating much."

He ate some more chicken. If he said what was really on his mind, she'd run off crying. He figured the best thing to do was eat the lunch and tell her another day that he wasn't interested in her. Mary Lou would still be hurt, but it seemed almost cruel to tell her over the lunch that she'd gone to so much trouble to prepare.

When he finished eating, he said, "Well, *denke* for a lovely meal, Mary Lou. You didn't need to go to this much trouble, but I appreciate it."

"I enjoyed doing it for you. And perhaps we can ..."

"Like I said before at Levi's wedding, I'm really busy the next few weeks."

She pouted. "I know. That's why I made this lunch. You had time to have lunch, didn't you?"

He nodded.

"Well, I'm glad you enjoyed it."

"I did. And now I must get back to work. Can I help you take everything back to your buggy?" He knew she'd brought the table and the chairs as well.

"*Nee*, I can do it. You go back to work. I don't like to keep you since you're so busy." She stood up abruptly and started packing up the food, making it

38

very clear by the way she was pouting that she was upset.

"Look, Mary Lou, I appreciate your kindness in making this lunch."

She spun around to look at him. "And?"

"And … *denke.* Now I must get back to work."

"Jah, you go. I know how important your work is."

"I'll see you soon."

"Okay, bye."

"Bye, Mary Lou, and *denke."*

She gave him a strained smile before she turned away. He hurried back to the workshop, and on the way, he found Hazel in her office sipping a mug of steaming coffee.

He stuck his head through her doorway. "You could've warned me," he whispered.

"I'm sorry, but there wasn't much I could do. It was all last-minute."

He sighed. "Try to give me some warning if this kind of thing happens again."

"I will. I take it lunch didn't go so well?" Hazel asked.

"Nee. I've never liked surprises. Although, it was a kind thought."

Hazel nodded, and then he hurried back to start work. It hadn't been a break, not really. It had only made him tense, trying to skirt around the issue of his lack of feeling toward her. And indigestion was likely to follow ... He wanted to tell Mary Lou that he liked someone else and would never be interested in her— not in a gazillion years, but he was happy with his decision not to tell her his true feelings today. Hopefully, what he'd said had given her a big enough hint.

CHAPTER 6

As Joshua took up where he'd left off before lunch, his brothers returned from their usual haunt.

"Where were you?" Benjamin, his youngest brother, asked.

"I had lunch here."

"I saw Hazel calling you. What was all that about?"

He looked around and when he saw his other brothers weren't nearby, he answered, "It was Mary Lou. She'd made me lunch. She went to a lot of trouble."

"Made you lunch and brought it here?"

"Jah, as a surprise. Anyway, keep it to yourself."

"Who would I tell?"

"Everyone," Joshua answered.

"I won't. Your secret's safe with me." Benjamin gave him a wink.

"It's not like that. I don't like her. Not that way."

"What? Are you crazy? She's beautiful."

"She might be, but don't you think it's weird? I mean, she was dating Isaac for years and then she liked Levi, and now she's moved on to liking me?"

"She can't help it if she's got bad taste in men."

"Get out of here."

Benjamin laughed. "Hey, as long as you're not interested, do you think I'd have a chance?"

"There's no way in the world. You're way too young for her."

"You're younger than her, too."

"Yeah, but not by much. Not as much as you; now, get back to work."

Benjamin walked away.

He pitied the poor girl who ended up with Benjamin; at sixteen he had a lot of growing up to do. He had no idea about girls and seemed to like them all. He was a maverick, Joshua thought, but a goodhearted one.

ADELINE WAS PINNING out the last of the washing when she heard a buggy. Catherine would normally be helping her, but she was in bed with a bad cold. Their mother was out visiting and their father at work, so Adeline was left to do everything. She quickly pinned out the last dress and hurried to see who their visitor was. It was too early to be her mother back home as she'd only just left. When she got around to the other side of the house, she saw Mary Lou stepping down from the buggy.

"Hi, Mary Lou."

Since Mary Lou was older, she was on the outer fringe of Adeline's group of friends.

"Hi, Adeline. I've got the day off and I thought I'd stop by to see you."

"Great. Come inside. I've just finished hanging out the laundry and I can do with some company."

She took Mary Lou through to the kitchen and they both sat down at the kitchen table.

"Now, would you like hot tea or *kaffe?* Perhaps a cold drink?"

"Nee denke. I've just come from lunch."

"Okay. Then let's go sit in the living room." Adeline was pleased to have a visitor, and the reason was if Adeline's mother came home and complained that she hadn't gotten much work done, she could always tell her it was because Mary Lou interrupted her chores.

Once they were sitting on the comfortable couch, Mary Lou said, "You haven't asked me about my lunch."

"Where did you go?"

"I had lunch with Joshua."

Adeline's heart sank. "You did?" When she'd seen Mary Lou and Joshua talking at the wedding, she'd never dreamed he would've asked her out. Had Mary

Lou come there to boast? Did she know somehow that she liked him too?

"*Jah.* We had a cozy lunch not far from where he works. I can't wait to tell Nella."

"Why would you want to tell Nella?"

Mary Lou laughed. "Nella likes him. Surely you know that."

"I can't say what I know. I don't like it when talk gets around. If I say something, then someone will say I said it, and how they tell it might not be correct. *Dat* says that's gossip."

"Everyone knows Nella likes him and has liked him for ages. It's not gossip when it's a cold hard fact."

Mary Lou was speaking gruffly and Adeline was a little wary of her. She got the feeling that no one ever disagreed with Mary Lou without backlash.

"When did he ask you out for lunch? Was it at the wedding?"

Mary Lou's gaze traveled to the ceiling. "I can't remember. Oh, you've got cobwebs."

Adeline gasped. She hated cobwebs. That meant spiders. "Where?"

Mary Lou pointed to the corner of the room above the back door.

Pleased that she couldn't see any spiders in the web, Adeline said, "I'll get it down later." She looked back at Mary Lou. "I'm glad you had a nice lunch."

"Are you?" Mary Lou tipped her head back and her eyes glistened.

A shiver went down Adeline's spine. "Of course I am."

"I suppose you'd rather Nella be his girlfriend than me."

Adeline felt a pain shoot through her heart. She was calling herself 'his girlfriend.' Could it be true? All she wanted to do was throw herself on her bed and cry. "It doesn't matter to me."

"Really?"

"Joshua should have whoever he chooses."

"And who do you think Joshua's choice should be?" Mary Lou leaned forward and jutted out her chin.

A weird sensation flooded through Adeline's body as an urge to slap Mary Lou's face came over her. She'd never hit anyone in her life before. Not even her little sister when she'd been excruciatingly annoying. Adeline coughed hard in an effort to rid herself of the urge. "It's up to him. No one can speak for him. He needs to follow his heart."

"Hmm. You're very similar to Lucy. You even talk the same."

"Well, she is my *schweschder*. So, are you his girl-friend now?"

"I'm not far off it."

Relief washed over Adeline. She was pleased that he hadn't chosen a girlfriend yet, but at the same time, she didn't want to be in some kind of three-way race with Mary Lou and Nella.

Catherine appeared at the bottom of the stairs in her nightgown, clutching a well-loved rag doll. "Hello, Mary Lou."

Mary Lou turned around and looked at her. "Catherine, are you only just waking at this time of day?"

"She's got a bad cold," Adeline explained.

Catherine walked a few steps closer. "I just came down for water. I've drunk my whole pitcher. *Mamm* told me to drink a lot."

"Go back to bed. I'll refill it in a minute."

"Now please, Adeline. *Mamm* said I need to drink a lot to get rid of this cold."

"Okay, just go back and I'll bring more up."

"You're a bit old for dollies, aren't you?" Mary Lou smirked at Catherine.

Catherine walked over and sat next to Mary Lou. *"Nee,* I'm not. I'm going to sleep with this one forever." She hugged it to herself.

"She used to cry if anyone took it from her when she was a *boppli.* Our *grossmammi* made it for her before she died."

"Well, she couldn't have made it after she died." Mary Lou laughed, but no one else did. She edged herself away from Catherine. "Don't sit so close. I don't want to get ill. I'm too busy for that. I don't get paid for sick days."

Catherine coughed without covering her mouth and Mary Lou sprang to her feet. "I'll stop by another time, Adeline."

"Are you going already?" Adeline asked, as she too stood.

"*Jah.* It's my day off and I've got a lot to do. The day's nearly gone already."

Adeline walked Mary Lou to the door and then leaned her body against the side of the doorframe as she watched Mary Lou's horse and buggy head down the driveway.

"What did she want?" Catherine asked when Adeline finally closed the door.

"She told me she had lunch with Joshua. I think that's what she came here to tell me."

Catherine gasped. "I thought I heard her say Joshua's name. That's not good. What are you going to do?"

"I don't know. She implied she was his girlfriend, but when I asked her further questions, she said she was 'not far off' being his girlfriend."

"That means she's not at all and she's probably making the whole thing up."

"Do you think she made it up about having lunch with him?"

"She probably had lunch with him and lots of other people and she exaggerated the whole thing."

"I'll get you water." Adeline walked toward the kitchen.

"No need. I've got plenty."

She swung around and stared at her younger sister. "You told me you'd run out."

"I was helping you get rid of her." Catherine sneezed.

"That wasn't necessary. I can handle her."

"I'm not sure about that." Catherine wiped her nose on her sleeve.

"Yuck! Don't do that."

"I don't have any more handkerchiefs."

"Just go back to bed and I'll bring you some of *Dat's.* Do you want me to heat you up some soup?"

"*Jah* please, and I'd like some thick bread with loads of butter."

"You can't be too sick if you're that hungry."

Catherine started up the stairs and called out behind her, "Feed a cold and starve a fever. That's what they say."

Her sister's words went in one ear and out the other. Adeline was too concerned about what Mary Lou had told her. She knew she had to leave things be and not worry, but why had Mary Lou visited her and told her she'd had lunch with Joshua? Was she hoping that she would then tell Nella? That had to be it.

If Joshua had any feelings for her at all, Adeline thought as she was getting her sister's soup warmed, he wouldn't have had lunch with Mary Lou. That meant she'd misread his glances, had been wrong about him liking her. It was a horrible thing that the first man she'd ever liked didn't like her. She sat down at the kitchen table while a single tear trickled down her cheek.

CHAPTER 7

HOURS LATER, Adeline made the decision to visit Nella. She'd fed Catherine hot soup, brought in the washing that was already dry thanks to a westerly breeze, and had chopped all the vegetables in preparation for the evening meal. The rest she'd do when she got home. On the days her mother spent visiting, she never liked to cook when she got home. Adeline left a note for *Mamm* saying that she'd do everything to finish the meal preparations on her return.

When Adeline pulled her buggy up at Nella's parents' house, the front door opened immediately and instead of Nella standing in the doorway, it was Nella's mother.

Adeline secured her horse and buggy and then walked over to her.

"I'm so glad you've come, Adeline. Nella is so upset she's making herself sick."

"What's wrong?"

"Best you talk to her yourself. She's in her bedroom."

Adeline hurried to her friend's room, the last on the left down the narrow dark hallway. She knocked on the door when she found it closed.

"Who is it?" asked a small voice.

"Adeline."

"Come in."

She opened the door to see Nella sitting up in bed and wiping her eyes as she turned and swung her feet to the floor. "What's happened, Nella?"

"It's Mary Lou."

"What's she done?" Adeline wondered if she'd already heard about Mary Lou having lunch with Joshua.

"She and Joshua ..." She started crying.

"What? Don't be so upset." She rested a hand on Nella's shoulder.

Nella took a deep breath. "She and Joshua had lunch."

"*Jah,* I know. She stopped by my *haus* to tell me today. How did you hear about it?"

"Because Mrs. Dalton saw Mary Lou there, where Joshua works. She was there getting a pantry door replaced. Mary Lou told her she was having lunch with

Joshua. Mrs. Dalton told *Mamm.*"

"Oh. Well, it mightn't be as bad as it sounds."

"It is. It is, I'm sure of it. What about how they were talking for so long at the wedding?"

"That doesn't mean anything. They were just talking. It's not as if they've announced their marriage."

"Don't even say that!"

When Adeline looked into her friend's red, tear-smattered face, she knew she could never have Joshua. Not with Mary Lou liking him and now Nella being so fixated on him.

"I'm happy you came here," Nella said sniffing back tears.

"I don't like to see you so upset."

"I won't be if you help me."

"Help with what?" Adeline asked.

"I have a plan. A plan to make Joshua my boyfriend. Will you help me? I need your help."

If she couldn't marry Joshua, she wanted it to be Nella who married him. Mary Lou needed a strong-willed man who wouldn't let her control him. "Okay, I suppose. What is it?"

Nella sniffed. "I've been thinking while I've been sitting here alone. I can't just do nothing. I have to try something. You know how the three oldest Fuller boys help the elderly and the widows around their houses every Friday afternoon?"

"*Jah.*"

"Well, my old *Onkel* Trevor needs things done."

"Does he?"

"Not really." Nella managed a little giggle. "But he could, if you get my meaning."

Adeline twirled her prayer *kapp* strings around her finger. She didn't like to be drawn into deception. "Oh, I see. And if the Fuller boys go out to your *onkel's* farm, you'll be there?"

"Jah, but it won't be all three of the Fuller boys who go. I'll make sure that it's just Joshua who goes there."

"How are you going to do that?"

"Well, that's where you're going to have to come in," Nella said.

"Go on."

"Since your *schweschder* just married Levi, and Hazel is married to Isaac, Levi's *bruder,* that sort of makes you and Hazel related."

"I guess so."

"Can you ask her to arrange that it's just Joshua who goes to my *onkel's* place? I know for a fact that Hazel is the one who organizes their Friday afternoons."

"Okay, I can ask."

"Denke, Adeline. *Denke* so much!"

"Can I tell her why? She might do it for love—in the interest of love."

"Okay. Tell her whatever you have to. I just hope my plan works."

"Me too. When do you want to do it? This Friday?"

"*Jah.*"

"I don't know how I'll get to talk to Hazel before then."

"Stop by her work."

Adeline gulped. She didn't want Joshua to see her there, at his work.

"Unless you want to stop by her *haus,* but Isaac will be there and he'll hear everything."

Adeline scratched her forehead. "*Nee,* that wouldn't be good."

"So, you'll do it?"

Reluctantly, Adeline agreed. She felt she had no other choice.

WHEN ADELINE GOT HOME, she fixed everything for dinner and then, before her father got home, she ran a plate of food up the stairs to Catherine.

Catherine was sitting up in bed propped up by pillows.

"You're awake."

"*Jah.* The only way I can breathe is to sit up like this. What's going on?"

"You'll never guess what happened, and what I have to do."

"What?"

"I'll be back after dinner and I'll tell you everything."

Adeline resisted Catherine's pleas and hurried back down the stairs to set the table for dinner.

Throughout dinner, Adeline heard about her mother's visitings.

Then her mother stopped and put her fork down. "What's wrong?"

"Nothing."

"You've barely said two words."

Adeline could've said she couldn't get two words in because her mother hadn't stopped to take a breath, but she would've earned a reprimand from her father if she'd said that.

"What did you and Catherine do today?"

She wrinkled her nose and looked over at her father who was silently cutting up the meat on his plate. "Catherine stayed home in bed, and I ..."

"*Jah,* I know you went out. You didn't rub the horse down properly and he was in the wrong paddock."

"Oh, I'm sorry."

"Well, what was so important that you left your *schweschder* alone while she was sick?"

"I gave her soup and then she wanted to sleep. I didn't think it would hurt for me to go out if I did all my chores."

"Where did you go?" her mother asked again.

"I went to Nella's *haus.*"

"How is she?"

"Okay."

"Then why have you been so quiet?"

"Have I?"

"She might be coming down with the same virus Catherine's got," her father suggested.

Her mother stood up and leaned forward and held the back of her hand to Adeline's forehead. *"Nee,* she doesn't feel hot."

"I feel okay. I'm just in a quiet mood." She was relieved when her mother and father started talking to one another and stopped talking about her.

"You know who I'm trying to get friendly with?" her mother asked her father.

"Who?" he replied.

"Hazel's mother. She keeps to herself and she's very shy, but she needs friends. She hasn't made one single friend since she's been here."

"And you'll be her friend?" her father asked in an amused tone.

"Jah. I feel sorry for her. Things have never gone well for her. I like her. She seems nice and you can never have too many friends. I'll visit her soon. Will you come with me, Adeline?"

Adeline had been thinking about Joshua and when she heard her name, she looked up, not too happy about being involved in conversation. She just wanted to feel sorry for herself in silence. "Sure. I'll visit her with you."

"Good. I've heard she's a little depressed and there's

nothing like a young person to lift someone's spirits." She leaned forward toward Adeline. "You'll have to get out of this mood. We can't visit her while you're like this."

"I'll be fine. I'm just a little tired today."

"I think we should visit her this coming Saturday afternoon."

"*Jah, Mamm.*"

CHAPTER 8

JOSHUA FELT awful about the dreadful lunch he'd had with Mary Lou. Well, a good lunch, but with a dreadful companion. He hadn't believed his eyes when he'd seen her there with that table full of food. Hazel had assured him she'd had nothing to do with it and she'd been caught up in the whole thing at the last minute.

He sat down at the dinner table with his four younger brothers. Now that he was the eldest son living at home, he knew he had to set a good example for the others.

ADELINE WAITED until lunchtime the next day before she went to the Fuller's factory.

She hoped Hazel was having her lunch there. She parked the buggy as close as she could to the door and walked into the factory. All she saw was an open factory until she walked a few more steps and then she saw two glass-walled offices off to one side. There Hazel was, in one of the offices behind a computer. She hurried to the door and knocked on it.

"Adeline. Come in." Hazel sprang to her feet.

"I hope you don't mind me stopping by."

"Of course not. Have a seat."

When Adeline was seated, Hazel sat also.

"The reason I'm here is I have a huge favor to ask you. It's not for myself it's for someone else."

"I'll help if I can."

"It's to do with Nella. Everyone knows that you arrange Isaac and Levi, and also Joshua, to help people in the community on Friday afternoons."

"*Jah?*"

"Nella was hoping that you would organize Joshua to go to her *Onkel* Trevor's place on this Friday afternoon."

"*Jah,* I'll just write that down. What does he need done?"

Adeline looked down. "Is it possible to arrange that Joshua goes there alone?"

Hazel stared at her. "Why's that?"

"Because Nella wants to be alone with him."

Hazel's brow furrowed "Wants to be alone with her *onkel?*"

"Nee, nee. She wants to be alone with Joshua, if you get my meaning."

"Ach, I see."

"Do you think you'd be up to doing that?"

"Hmmm. Only if her *Onkel* Trevor needs something done. Otherwise, I'm just sending my *bruder*-in-law on a blind date."

Adeline nodded. *"Jah,* I'm sure there's something that needs to be done there. And then Nella would just happen to show up. I don't like asking but …"

"It's okay. I can do that. I'll find out from Nella what needs to be done at her *onkel's haus.* Anyway, with Levi away this week, I was planning on sending the two of them to some of the places separately anyway."

"Were you?"

Hazel nodded.

"Denke so much, Hazel. I was hoping you would do it. I didn't like asking. I feel a bit awkward about the whole thing."

"It's okay, don't let it bother you." Then she said, "I packed more than enough lunch for just myself today if you'd like to stay and share it with me?"

"Denke, but I need to get back home, and I didn't want any of the Fuller boys to see me here."

"I understand. Why don't you stop by the *haus* and visit me sometime?"

"I'd like that. Do you work every day?"

"*Jah,* I work the usual five days, and sometimes a Saturday morning."

"I'll remember that, and I'll stop by one weekend in the afternoon, or you could come and visit us. *Mamm* and Catherine would enjoy it, too." Adeline didn't mention her mother's plans, knowing *Mamm* wanted the visit the next day to be seen as spontaneous.

Adeline left the Fullers' workshop pleased with her interaction with Hazel. She was so sweet the way she had offered to share her lunch.

It was Friday afternoon and, for some reason unknown to Joshua, it had been organized that he visit Trevor Yoder alone. That was odd because he normally went with his two older brothers, and that way they got their jobs done in a third of the time and then they'd go onto the next.

Hazel was insistent that he go to old Trevor Yoder's by himself, saying that since Levi was away Isaac and he would get things done quicker if they split up. She also said that Trevor's job was a job for one, and now that she was organizing their Friday afternoons, he didn't like to disagree. The system they already had in place worked, though, so why change it? He was glad that things would return to normal once Levi was back. It was more enjoyable working side-by-side with his brothers.

He jumped down from his wagon as soon as he arrived at Trevor's house. Once he had wound the reins around the post, he made his way to the house to have a word with Trevor before he fixed the hole in his barn, and to see if there was anything else that needed doing.

He knocked on the door, and was surprised that Nella answered it.

"Nella! I didn't expect to see you here."

"*Onkel* Trevor said to tell you he's sorry he wasn't here, and he wanted me to show you where the hole in the barn is."

"Okay."

She stepped out of the house and closed the door behind her. He wondered whether this was another set-up. It had to be. That's something he'd take up with Hazel. If he finished early he'd have a word with her today. Otherwise, it would have to wait until the very next morning. Everyone was working on this Saturday morning due to the large order of kitchenettes for a hotel. They had to finish them for delivery during the following week.

She headed down the porch steps and then turned around to face him. "I suppose you're looking forward to getting married now that your two older brothers are married?"

"Not especially."

"Well, I mean, you're around the age to get married."

"Hazel didn't say if anything else needs doing here."

"There's just the hole in the barn. Follow me. I'll show you." She pulled open the double doors of the barn and led him through to the back of one of the horse stalls. "One of his horses kicked it in."

"Where's your *onkel* today?"

"He was going to be here, but he got called away somewhere. Do you need to wait until he comes back before you can fix it?"

"*Nee.* I've got wood in the wagon that I can patch this with. It won't take too long. If he was here, I would've had a talk with him about how he wanted it done."

"I'm sure whatever you do will be fine."

"Okay. I'll just get the wood and my tools." He walked out of the barn with her following him close behind.

"Do you mind if I watch you work?"

"It doesn't bother me."

She giggled. "Maybe I can help."

"It's okay, I won't need any help. It's just a small job."

He made two trips from the wagon with his tools and the wood he needed for the repair. All the while, Nella followed talking to him. He measured the wood and then took hold of his saw to cut it.

"I'm ready to get married," she said suddenly, just as he was about to start sawing.

He froze, and looked up at her in shock. "Oh."

"Do you know anyone who might be interested?"

"There might be a lot of men, you just have to find someone that's compatible."

"Maybe I already have."

He nodded. "That's good."

"Joshua, I'm talking about you."

He gulped. "Me?" All he wanted to do was finish the repair and get out of the place. Since it was a small job, he'd left it until last.

"*Jah,* you."

He had to be honest. "Nella, I'm sorry. I'm flattered, and I think you're nice, but I don't feel that way about you." Her face twisted as though she were in pain. He continued, "I don't know why I feel that way, I just do."

"Maybe it's because you don't really know me. Perhaps if we spend some more time together—"

That was something he couldn't do because the only woman he wanted to spend time with was Adeline. "I already have a girl I like."

"You do?"

He nodded.

"Who is it?"

"I'd rather not say at the moment." He looked back down and sawed the wood and when he looked up again, Nella had gone.

The last thing he wanted was to hurt her feelings, but the kindest thing he could do was tell her the truth.

After the hole was repaired and his tools were back in his wagon, he knocked on the door and Nella opened it just slightly.

"All done," he said.

"Denke," said a small voice. "Bye."

"Bye, Nella."

Instead of going home, Joshua hurried back to work. It was just before five, so Hazel would still be there. The best thing was to nip this in the bud, before it blew out of proportion. He didn't want talk to get around about him and Nella, or him and Mary Lou. This was the second time Hazel had caused him to get into hot water.

He found Hazel sitting in her office tapping away at a calculator. She looked up at him, surprised to see him back there so late on a Friday afternoon.

"Hazel, why did you put me on the roster to go to Trevor Yoder's?"

"Well ... I thought it best because ... I already told you it was a small job and Levi wasn't here to do the usual thing of you all going together."

He could tell by the way she looked away from him that there was more to it. She was embarrassed by something and she was clearly keeping something from him. "Come on, Hazel. You can tell me the rest. I know you were forced into it. I've only come here to ask you not to do anyone any favors again. First it was Mary Lou and now you did a favor for Nella." He couldn't blame her. She was fairly new to their community and she probably just wanted friends. That was why it was difficult for her to say no to people. The thing was, she had to know not to do it again.

"You've got it wrong it. It wasn't Nella, it was Adeline who asked me."

His heart beat faster when he heard her name. "Adeline?"

"Jah. She asked me if you could go alone to Trevor Yoder's. I guess that's the same thing, though. I'm sorry. I won't be drawn into anything again. And please don't say anything to Adeline."

"Denke for telling me, Hazel. I wonder why she would want me to do that."

"It's obvious."

He stared at Hazel. "Is it?"

"She was only helping her friend."

He was upset by that news. After he'd given Hazel a sharp nod, he stepped out of her office and came face-to-face with Jacob.

"So, your Adeline isn't as sweet as you'd like to think? *And* she doesn't like you."

Joshua didn't want to entertain the thought of Adeline not liking him. "I don't know how you could say that."

"I overheard all of it. If Adeline was helping Nella be alone with you that means she doesn't like you at all."

It didn't fit with the woman he knew Adeline was. He'd have to confront her and ask her if she'd done it. Somehow, Hazel must've been mistaken. Joshua shook his head. "I won't hear anything bad about Adeline."

"I wouldn't call it bad. Like Hazel said, she was helping her friend. That's admirable."

"I wish you wouldn't listen in all the time. It's very bad manners." Joshua took a deep breath. He couldn't bear it if Adeline was helping one of her friends win his heart. He didn't like to admit Jacob might be right, but it followed that, if Adeline had schemed with Nella, Adeline couldn't like him.

Jacob said, "If I were you, I'd give some attention to Mary Lou."

"Really?" Joshua could scarcely believe his ears. "Why Mary Lou?"

"I heard how she surprised you with lunch."

"You heard?"

"Jah. I'd love it if a girl did that for me."

Joshua chuckled. "You told me you're irresistible to women, and now you tell me no girl's done anything like that for you?"

Jacob's lips downturned. "That would only be because they wouldn't know if I'd like it or not."

"Whatever you say."

"Anyway, I wouldn't rule out Mary Lou just because she liked Isaac and then Levi."

"She's going down the line, isn't she? You'll be next."

Joshua immediately felt bad about joking that way about Mary Lou. If she found out they were talking about her like that she'd be crushed by embarrassment. "Mary Lou's a nice girl, but she's not for me."

"Hmm. She should've skipped you and gone straight to me. That would've saved us all some bother. Adeline doesn't care for you, and who can blame her? She's way too young."

"I'll wait."

Jacob gave Joshua a brotherly slap on his back. "It doesn't matter how long you wait. You'll still be that much older, and I don't think Adeline's the way you think she is."

"And what's that?"

"Innocent and sweet."

"She is."

Jacob raised an eyebrow. "We'll see."

"Just forget it. Leave things be."

CHAPTER 9

MRS. MILLER LOOKED over at Adeline on Saturday morning. "Don't forget, this afternoon, we're going to visit Hazel and her *mudder.* I don't like to leave Catherine for too long while she's still sick, so we'll have to be quick, and did I mention Catherine wants pumpkin bread?"

"I'll make her some. Do we have a recipe for it in *Mammi's* box?"

"Nee. Go to the markets for me. Gracie sells pumpkin bread at her stall. I hope she has some today. If she doesn't, you should be able to find some somewhere else, at one of the other stalls."

Adeline knew what was coming next. Her mother was going to ask her to go to the markets by herself. "You want me to go alone?"

"Good idea, *denke*. That'll give me a chance to do some things around here while you're gone."

Adeline walked outside and said goodbye to her father who was finishing off painting a small table by the barn. As well as working every weekday, her father worked every second Saturday.

He slowly straightened himself up. "Where are you off to?"

"*Mamm* wants me to get something for Catherine."

"Herbs for that nasty cold?"

"*Nee*, pumpkin bread."

"Where are you going for that?"

"The farmers market."

His mouth turned down at the corners. "You're going all the way there for that?"

"*Jah.*"

"Just that one thing?"

"That's right."

"Does your *Mamm* know?"

"She's the one who's sending me."

He shook his head. "Is Catherine any better?"

"About the same."

Her father grunted and Adeline silently agreed with her father. It was a waste of time and money going to the markets for one thing. "Do you want anything while I'm there?"

He shook his head. "I'll hitch the buggy for you."

"*Nee, Dat.* I'll do it. You carry on with your painting."

"All right. I like to finish a painting job once I start. That way the brush stays good. With this heat, it'd dry out if I left it too long."

Adeline nodded and headed to the paddock to fetch the black horse. Midnight was their main buggy horse. The other one was Bonnie, and he was old now, nearly ready for retirement.

WHILE ADELINE WALKED Midnight along the roads, she missed having one of her sisters by her side. Normally, Catherine or Lucy went everywhere with her. Now that Lucy was married, that left only Catherine to keep her company. It wasn't long before her thoughts turned to Joshua. Images of Nella and Joshua at Nella's uncle's place buzzed around in her mind. She didn't exactly know what Nella had planned for yesterday. One part of her wanted things to work out for her friend, but another part of her wanted Joshua to reject Nella's advances. She wanted Joshua for herself.

If she gave Joshua one little bit of encouragement, however, or even if she smiled at him, she felt she'd be betraying her friend. Sighing, Adeline looked out over the patchwork of green fields as she went by them. Joshua was even further away from her and seemed to get further away yet with every passing day. Even if

Joshua liked her, it wouldn't be right because if she and Joshua became a couple it would upset Nella too much. Then she realized she should've been more upfront with Nella and told her that she liked Joshua too. That would've been the sensible thing to do.

JUST AS SHE pulled the buggy into the parking lot of the markets, she saw another buggy and a tall bay horse. At first, she thought it was Joshua standing by the horse talking to an *Englisch* girl and her heart nearly stopped. Looking closer, she saw it was his brother, Jacob. Jacob turned around and looked at her, as did the girl he was talking with. Then Jacob said something to the girl, she said something to him, and then the girl walked away.

Jacob waited until Adeline got out of the buggy before he made his way over to her. "Hello, Adeline."

"Hi, Jacob."

"What brings you here?"

"My *schweschder* is sick and she's got a hankering for pumpkin bread."

He chuckled. "Wait, Lucy's sick?"

"*Nee,* it's Catherine. I don't think Lucy's back until tomorrow or maybe the next day."

"*Jah,* that's right. What's wrong with Catherine?"

Adeline got down from the buggy. "Just a cold, or the flu. I don't think it's anything serious, but I sure hope Lucy didn't catch it before their travels."

"You came all the way here for bread?"

"I know it's a bit weird." While they talked, she wondered who the *Englisch* girl was. Had he been flirting with her? From the beaming look on the girl's face, it seemed so. He was handsome, that was for certain. Lots of the girls in the community liked him, but more liked Joshua.

"What kind of bread did you say?"

"Pumpkin bread."

"It must be some pumpkin bread to make you travel all this way."

"Mamm thinks so. It's not too far to come here. Anyway, sometimes when you're sick your body calls out for a certain type of food and Catherine's is calling out for pumpkin bread."

"I have never been sick enough to know about anything like that."

She finished securing her horse and wondered why he was still sticking around. After an awkward silence, he said, "I'm glad we ran into each other, I wanted to talk to you about something."

"Jah?"

"Don't take this the wrong way, but I don't think it's nice to use Hazel in the way that you did."

"What do you mean?" She could tell by his face he was very upset.

"She's fairly new here and she wants to make friends and I think you used her to do your bidding."

"What bidding? I don't know what you're talking about. I haven't done anything."

"You forced Hazel to arrange it so Joshua would be alone with Nella at her *onkel's haus*."

Embarrassed, Adeline looked down on the ground. "Oh."

"It's true?"

Adeline nodded. "It's true that I asked her if she could. I didn't force her."

"Hazel should not be taken advantage of like that. She has been through so much in her life. My family feels protective of her, you need to understand that."

"Jah, I've heard what she's been through. I didn't mean to do anything wrong."

"Well you did. You took advantage of her and I don't want it to happen again."

"It won't. I'll never do anything like that again." Adeline was very upset with Nella for asking her do it. But as Adeline's father often said, she couldn't blame anyone else; she had to take responsibility for her own actions. "I feel dreadful. Did I upset Hazel?"

"Jah, you did."

"That's the last thing I wanted to do."

"Maybe you should apologize."

"I definitely will." She bit her lip, hoping he wouldn't also suggest to apologize to Joshua. That would be too embarrassing. *"Mamm* and I are visiting her this afternoon, so I'll definitely apologize then. *Denke* for bringing it to my attention."

"I shouldn't have had to."

Adeline looked down at the ground again not knowing what to say. She felt like she was being reprimanded by her father which was odd because Jacob was not that much older than herself. "I didn't think it would upset Hazel at all. It really wasn't that big of a deal."

"Manipulating people is a big deal."

She raised her eyebrows. *Manipulating?* She wondered what Hazel had said to him and what Hazel said to Joshua, for that matter. Hopefully, she would find out that afternoon when she saw Hazel. "I'll talk to Hazel and make amends. Don't worry."

He nodded. "See that you do, or I'll have to take things further. Bishop John and Ruth are very protective of Hazel also."

Now he'd made her mad. There was no need to threaten to tell the bishop. Besides, she'd done nothing wrong. It had seemed harmless to ask Hazel if she could send Joshua to Nella's uncle's place alone. Many women, and men for that matter, played matchmaker, there was nothing wrong with it.

"Did you know that *Englischer* you were talking to just now?" Adeline couldn't resist having a little dig at him.

He moved uncomfortably from one foot to the other. "Why do you ask?"

"Her skirt was very short and she didn't look like the kind of girl your parents would be happy with you talking to, or for that matter, neither would the bishop."

"I see what you're trying to do."

"I'm just asking a question. Anyway, I've just gotta get this pumpkin bread back to my *schweschder.*" She flounced past him, no longer worried by what he thought. He sure was handsome, but he wasn't nice like Joshua. *The nerve of him, threatening to go to the bishop over something so trivial.* If she truly had upset Hazel, she'd apologize to her and that would be the end of the matter.

CHAPTER 10

WHEN ADELINE GOT inside the farmers market, she glanced over her shoulder and saw Jacob climb into his buggy, and then she watched him leave. She'd never been good at confrontations. Sure, she'd had lots of squabbles with her two sisters, but that was different. She'd never before been made to feel like she was feeling right now, and it made her sick to her stomach.

Doing her best to put the whole incident out of her mind, she headed to find the stall her mother had told her about—Gracie Stofzuz's.

She finally found the stall and Gracie had two loaves of pumpkin bread left. Adeline bought both of them, and told Gracie, "Catherine's sick and all she wants to eat is pumpkin bread. I'm so glad you still have some."

"What's wrong with her?"

"Just a cold, we think."

"I hope these make her feel better." She beamed a smile at Adeline. "I'll slip a couple of cookies in for her, too, and one for you." Gracie gave Adeline a wink.

"*Ach, denke.*" Gracie's kind gesture made up for the altercation she'd had with Jacob Fuller just moments before.

Gracie handed over the brown paper bag, a sturdy one with string handles.

"*Denke,* Gracie, and for the cookies also."

Gracie giggled. "Tell your *schweschder* I hope she gets better soon."

"I will. Bye."

"Bye now, Adeline."

Now Adeline was faced with the long drive home, pleased she had a cookie to munch on. She walked along the stalls looking straight ahead. The last thing she needed was to see something she wanted to buy because she had very little money left. Just as she reached the exit, a whiff of freshly ground coffee grabbed her attention. She stepped away from the bustling crowd, stopped, and inhaled deeply. Coffee was one of her favorite smells. She followed the aroma into the café and treated herself to a take-out coffee for the way home. The change from the bread exactly covered the money for the coffee. And a coffee would go so nicely with her cookie.

When she reached the buggy, she climbed in and

then arranged her coffee where it was safe from spilling but she could access it easily. Then Adeline made her way out of the parking lot. As she munched her cookie, listening to the rhythmic clip-clopping of her horse's hooves, she understood why many people found peace in solitude. The silence soothed her. If she ended up living alone one day, it wouldn't be so bad.

Glancing down at her coffee, she figured it would've cooled enough to take a sip. When she saw a smooth patch of road ahead, she carefully drank a little. If she got coffee down her dress she'd have to change it before they went to visit Hazel and her mother. Monday was washing day and since it was Saturday, she only had one clean dress—her best dress—and she was saving that for Sunday.

When she arrived home, she was pleased that she didn't need to unhitch the buggy. They'd use it again when they went to Hazel's. Adeline drained the rest of the coffee and placed the cardboard cup in the trashcan by the barn, and then she carried the bag with the pumpkin bread and Catherine's cookies into the house.

She opened the door and saw Catherine lying on the couch wrapped in a blanket. "How do you feel?"

"Okay. A little better today. Did you get my bread?"

"Jah." She held up the bag. "And Gracie put two cookies in for you."

"That was kind of her. Did you tell her I'm sick?"

"Jah. Where are *Mamm* and *Dat?"*

"In the kitchen getting something to eat, I think."

"How do you want your bread? Warmed up?"

"Jah, with loads of butter, please. And could you make me a hot tea? I'll have the cookies now, *denke."*

Adeline gave her the bag with the cookies and then headed to the kitchen forgoing the lecture to her sister about eating so much butter. She was sure it wasn't good, but whatever she said to her sister went in one ear and out the other.

"There you are," her mother said when she walked into the kitchen. Her father and mother were both sitting at the kitchen table eating soup. "I thought we'd have lunch, and then we'd leave."

"Okay. I'll heat up some of the bread for Catherine."

"While it's heating you can eat your soup."

Adeline cut some pumpkin bread and placed it under the griller and then ladled herself some soup. She ate it quickly, so she could tell Catherine about what had happened with Jacob Fuller and what he'd said to her. She had to tell someone and she couldn't tell her parents because they'd find out about Nella and her and Mary Lou all liking Joshua. That would be a mess!

She sat there listening to her parents talk about what her father needed to do around the house—odd jobs and repairs and such. When Adeline had finished the small bowl of soup she'd served herself, she jumped up to take Catherine her warmed bread. Firstly, she spread it with lashings of butter and then she remembered the hot tea Catherine had requested. Hoping her sister wouldn't remember about the tea, she took the bread to her.

"Here you are."

"*Denke.* This looks good."

She sat down beside Catherine, looked back to make sure her parents were still in the kitchen, and then whispered, "You'll never guess what happened today."

"What?" Catherine munched into her hot buttered bread.

"I ran into Jacob Fuller at the markets and he told me off for involving Hazel in getting Joshua to Nella's *onkel's.*"

"What's it got to do with him?"

"He said Hazel was upset or something."

"About?"

Adeline sighed. "I suppose it was wrong to get someone else involved and I didn't want to. I only did it because I wanted to keep Nella happy. I'll talk to Hazel today and find out why it upset her so much."

Catherine swallowed what was in her mouth. "Good idea."

"And, Jacob was a bit mean and kind of threatened that he'd tell the bishop what I did."

Catherine's eyes opened wide. *"Nee!"*

"Jah, and it wasn't even that big of a deal, so I said

something about him speaking to an *Englisch* girl. I saw him talking to her when I pulled up at the markets."

Catherine giggled. "He wouldn't have liked that."

"He didn't."

"He should keep out of things."

"I guess he was only being protective of his *schweschder*-in-law. She has been through a hard time."

"With her mother being in a mental home?"

"They don't call it that these days, but *jah*. She was only there for a short while, but she's not a well woman and she and Hazel have been through a lot because of Hazel's *vadder*. Her mother still doesn't mix very well with people. That's why *Mamm's* trying to befriend her."

Catherine sighed. *"Mamm's* so good. I wonder if I can be like that someday."

Adeline giggled. "You will be. Just eat your bread."

"Well, if you stop talking to me I will."

Adeline leaned over and kissed Catherine on the forehead and Catherine pulled away. "Stop."

Adeline giggled again. "Okay. *Mamm* and I are going soon, so you can have some peace."

"Good. And before you go can you get me another piece of this?" Catherine held up a piece of pumpkin bread with butter dripping off it. "And the hot tea you forgot?"

"Okay. Don't get any of that butter on the couch."

"You already sound like *Mamm*."

Adeline swung around and her mouth fell open.

Catherine giggled. "Don't worry, I won't."

Adeline continued walking to the kitchen, glad that her sister was being cheeky because that meant she truly was feeling better.

CHAPTER 11

Joshua pushed the back door open on Saturday afternoon in serious need of food. He'd spent nearly the whole day oiling the leather sections of all the family's buggy harnesses. Once he was in the mudroom, he kicked off his boots, and then soaped up his hands and rinsed them thoroughly. Then he continued into the kitchen to see if he could find something to eat to hold him over until the evening meal.

He stopped in his tracks when he saw his mother slumped over the kitchen table crying. He rushed to her. *"Mamm,* what's wrong?"

"It's Timothy. He's leaving for his *rumspringa* tonight."

"You've known this has been coming for a while."

She nodded. "He's going with John Stoltzfus. They're both going together."

"It'll be good that he knows someone."

Timothy was the first of his brothers to go on *rumspringa*. Timothy had also given notice at the family's joinery factory that he was leaving. He wanted to see if he could make it on his own in the *Englisch* world.

"What if he never comes back?" she asked.

"You can't worry about things that haven't happened yet. Anyway, that's his choice to make. No one can make that choice for him."

"I know." She sobbed into her hands.

"I don't like to see you upset like this." He couldn't remember the last time he saw his mother cry. He'd seen her shed a tear at funerals, but that was all. Nothing like this.

"Wait until you have *kinner* of your own. Then you'll be able to understand. If I'd had a girl she would have been close to me."

"All of us boys are close to you, *Mamm.*"

She sniffed and looked up at him. "I've been waiting for one of you to marry a nice girl, someone I can think of as my *dochder,* but Isaac married Hazel and then Levi married Lucy."

"And they're lovely girls. You should give them more of a chance."

Hazel had come from a broken home, and *Mamm* had never liked the Millers, Lucy and Adeline's family. It had something to do with an uncle of theirs, he thought.

"Just tell me you'll marry a *gut* girl from a nice *familye*."

Now he was in an awkward situation. "*Mamm*, Hazel and Lucy are nice girls."

"I just wanted girls who I could feel were like my own *dochders*." She cried some more. "That's all I ask. I just want *Gott* to give me a nice *dochder*-in-law. I'm too old to have more *kinner* now. I've only ever wanted a *dochder*. Why am I being punished?" She sobbed uncontrollably and for the first time, Joshua felt he had to step into the role of the oldest son.

It made him uneasy to see his mother crying so hard. She was normally such a strong woman. "Everything will be okay. You'll love the girl I marry."

Her crying lessened. "Will I?"

"*Jah.* Now cheer up, please."

"Who will you marry? Do you have someone in mind?"

He chuckled. "I have lots of girls on my mind."

She gave a little giggle. "Find a nice girl who'll fit in with the family and get along with everyone. Some families keep to themselves too much, if you know what I mean."

He nodded, knowing she was referring to Hazel and the problem with her mother. Hazel's mother barely left the house. "Can I get you something, *Mamm*? Can I make you a hot cup of tea?"

She frowned at him. "I'll make one for you."

"Nee, I'll do it."

"Nee, you sit and I'll get it." She sprang to her feet and in a moment, she had the gas stove lit and the teakettle filled and sitting atop.

He didn't want to upset his mother, but he feared she'd definitely be upset if he married Adeline.

When she sat down again, he said, "Don't worry about Timothy, he'll be fine. He's probably the most sensible one out of all of us. He was born with the brain of a forty-year-old."

His mother chuckled. "That's true. He was always serious. I just hope he returns to us."

"Of course he will. He just wants to see what life's like before his baptism; that's what *rumspringa's* for. He won't stay away for long, I'm sure of it."

"I hope not. Now just tell me again that you'll marry a girl from a good family."

He studied his mother's face. "What has Timothy got to do with me marrying a good girl?"

"Nothing. These are the things that have been on my mind, and when I'm upset they all whirl in my head." She made circular motions with her hand above her head.

"I will, *Mamm.* I'll marry someone you like."

She smiled and patted his hand. "I knew you were one son I could rely on. You've always been reliable, even when you were a little *bu.*"

CHAPTER 12

As ADELINE'S mother drove the buggy to Hazel's house, Adeline asked, "Do they know we're coming?"

Her mother turned to look at her. "I didn't say anything to anyone, did you?"

Adeline shook her head. She'd avoided mentioning it to Hazel yesterday just in case plans had to be changed. It wasn't unusual for the Amish to stop by one another's houses without notice. Most everyone did that from time to time.

"I only hope they'll be home," her mother said.

"We can always stop by another time if they're not."

As they drove up to Isaac and Hazel's house, they saw clothes on the line. "It looks like someone's home," Adeline said.

"It does."

After they had secured the horse, they walked

together to the front door. Hazel's mother lived in the attached *grossdaddi haus*. She'd come to live with them not long after Isaac and Hazel married.

Hazel answered the door with a beaming smile on her face. "It's nice to see you. Come in." She stepped aside and both of them walked in.

"Would your *mudder* be home?" Mrs. Miller asked.

"*Jah*, she is."

"Would you mind if I knock on her door?"

"She'd love to see you."

"Good. I'll leave Adeline with you while I visit with her."

Just like that, Adeline was left alone with Hazel. It was the perfect opportunity to inquire about why Jacob was so upset.

"I just made some fresh lemonade, would you like some?"

"I sure would." Adeline followed Hazel to the kitchen and watched her pour two glasses of lemonade.

"Let's sit in the living room." Once they were seated on a blue couch by a large window, Hazel asked, "Where's Catherine?"

"She's sick at home. I'm so glad to get out of the *haus*."

Hazel gasped. "Nothing contagious, is it?"

Adeline giggled. "It's just a cold. Although, I guess a cold is contagious, but the rest of the family hasn't caught it from her. She's probably just pretending so she'll get out of chores and cause everyone to fuss over her."

"Oh good. I really don't want to get sick. I mean, I feel sorry for Catherine, if she's really sick."

"I'm glad we got this chance to talk because there's something I've been wanting to ask you."

"What is it?"

"Denke for what you did the other day for Nella ..."

Hazel studied her face. "Did it go horribly wrong for Joshua and Nella?"

Adeline shook her head. "I'm not certain. I haven't spoken to Nella about it. It's nothing like that, but did I upset you by asking you to arrange for Joshua to go by himself?"

"Nee, why?"

"I was at the farmers markets this morning and I ran into Jacob and he tore strips off me for asking you to do that. And I feel dreadful because I thought that was just between you and me. Why did you tell Jacob?"

"It wasn't like that." Hazel's voice quavered a little as she spoke.

Immediately, Adeline saw that Hazel's eyes brimmed with tears. She felt dreadful for upsetting her, and if she got upset so easily, now she could understand why Jacob was so defensive of her. "Oh, I feel dreadful, Hazel. It doesn't matter. It's not important, don't be upset."

Hazel put both hands up to her face and sobbed.

Adeline moved closer and put her arm around Hazel's shoulders. "I'm just a stupid girl. Don't worry about me." Tears came to Adeline's eyes as well.

Hazel stopped crying enough to speak. "That's not what I'm crying about. I'm pregnant."

"What?"

Hazel nodded. "I'm pregnant."

Adeline leaned back. "And you're not happy about it?"

"I'm so happy about it, and so is Isaac. We haven't told anyone yet because the first person we told was my *mudder,* and she's upset. She wants to leave and go back home where we used to live. We didn't even have a home there. We were living with my *aente* and *onkel.* This is the only home we've both had for the longest time—a proper home that is."

"What's your *mudder* upset about? I thought she'd be delighted to be a *grossmammi.*"

Hazel took a deep breath. "It's only been me and her for the longest time. We've only had each other to rely upon. She had a hard time at first with the idea of me marrying Isaac, and now she thinks the *boppli* will take all my attention and I won't want her around anymore."

"Ah, I see." Adeline didn't really understand, but she knew of Hazel's mother's fragile mental state.

"I should be happy at this time."

Adeline didn't know what to say to make her feel

better. Of course she should be happy, but how could she be happy if her mother wasn't? "Maybe my *mudder* can help in some way. Do you think your *mudder* will tell her what's going on?"

"I don't think so. She's so used to keeping everything bottled up inside. My *vadder* put us both through so much and we never told anybody how bad it was, not even to this day. Nobody but Isaac knows the half of it."

"I'm sorry to hear that, Hazel, very sorry. That must've been so hard for you. Where is your *vadder* now? Has he passed away?"

"He's got a new life and a new *Englisch* family now. He lives with another woman and her *kinner.*"

"Maybe your *mudder* needs to socialize more and do more activities and then she'll have her mind taken up with different things. Then she won't be so reliant on you."

"I know you're right. And I suggested that to her, but she doesn't want to do anything unless I go with her, and my work schedule makes that pretty difficult."

"That's hard."

Hazel nodded.

"You must be so excited about the *boppli.*"

"We're very excited, and Isaac wants to tell his family, but I don't want anybody else to know until *Mamm* is okay with it."

"I'm sorry for talking about my stupid problems."

"Nee don't be, and what you said isn't stupid. What did Jacob say to you?"

Adeline said, "Nothing, it doesn't matter anymore."

"Tell me. You can be sure I'm not upset with you at all. I'm really happy you came today."

Adeline shook her head. *"Nee.* There's no need to talk about Jacob. And I'm glad *Mamm* and I stopped in, too."

Hazel sighed. "I don't know what I'll do if my *mudder* goes home. I need her here, now more than ever. I know she'll be happy when the *boppli* comes. I only hope she stays here that long. She didn't send your *mudder* away just now, so that's a good sign."

"Would she have done that?"

"She's done that to people before." Hazel gave a little giggle. "I shouldn't laugh, it's not funny."

Hazel's problems made Adeline's worries look so small. She was ashamed of herself for even worrying about them. All her life, she'd taken for granted that she'd been raised in a good home with two loving parents. She hadn't even thought to thank God for that blessing. She silently prayed a prayer of thanks.

"I'm so happy for you Hazel—about your *boppli."*

"Me too. I mean, I want to be and I would be if it wasn't for my *mudder* being so upset."

Adeline put her arms around her and hugged her. "Your *Mamm* will tell my *Mamm* and my *mudder* will set her thinking straight."

"*Denke,* Adeline. I certainly hope so. I really don't want to be here alone. I mean, I know I've got Isaac and friends like you and Lucy, but my *mudder* and I are so close. There's nothing for her back there except painful memories. That's why she was happy for me to come here, and then she followed when I married."

"I'm glad you came here, and don't worry, everything will work out. *Gott* has a plan, a good plan."

"Isaac put so much work into making me a nice home here and building on the *grossdaddi haus* for *Mamm.*"

Adeline rubbed the side of her face. "She had to know you'd have *bopplis,* though."

"I don't think she gave it too much thought. It was probably a hazy thought—something that would happen in the distant future. Even I didn't think it would happen this fast."

CHAPTER 13

Two hours later, Adeline and Mrs. Miller were on the way home. Adeline still hadn't seen Hazel's mother. She hadn't come out of her little *grossdaddi haus* the whole time.

"What did you talk to Hazel's *mudder* about?"

"Just this and that. Nothing too exciting."

Adeline stared at her mother wondering whether Hazel's mother had confided in her or not. From the way her mother had clammed up, she guessed that they'd had a long conversation about everything. She hoped her mother was able to help her. They were halfway home, and still nothing was mentioned about Hazel's pregnancy. Adeline wasn't going to mention it, since none of the Fullers knew about it yet, except for Isaac.

"What did you and Hazel talk about?" her mother eventually asked.

"We had a nice glass of lemonade. She'd only just made it."

"Good. And what did you talk about?"

"It seems her *mudder* was a bit upset about something."

"Do you know what?"

Adeline could barely contain a smile. "You must've found out since you were talking with her *mudder*."

"Maybe I did."

"I hope you were able to give her some comfort."

Mrs. Miller nodded. *"Jah,* and I think the two of us will become good friends. We talked about many things."

"I'm glad." No more needed to be said. Adeline looked out across the fields feeling pleased she'd been there to give Hazel some comfort and that her mother had been able to talk with Hazel's mother.

Her good feelings didn't last long because when she and her mother arrived home, Nella's buggy was there. Then they saw Nella pacing up and down along the porch. Adeline knew instantly that Nella was upset and she silently made a good guess; her friend's mood was to do with Joshua.

"I think I need to talk with her in private, *Mamm.*"

Mrs. Miller sighed. "You girls and your boy troubles."

"How do you know it's boy troubles?"

"I used to be young once, you know. What else is there at your age? Go on, talk to her and I'll unhitch the buggy. Take as long as you want." Mrs. Miller's gaze traveled to the porch. "And from the looks of her, you're going to take some time."

"*Denke, Mamm.*"

Adeline climbed down from the buggy and Nella ran to meet her.

"Your *schweschder* wouldn't let me in the *haus*. She said she was sick. She wouldn't even let me wait in the living room."

Adeline shook her head at her sister's lack of social skills. "I'm sorry. She can be like that sometimes. Anyway, what's wrong?"

"How do you know something's wrong?"

Adeline whispered, "It's so obvious even my *mudder* could tell. I'm guessing things didn't go too well with Joshua. Didn't he show up at your *onkel's haus?*"

"He did, but I wish he hadn't."

Adeline glanced over at her mother who was now leading the horse closer to the barn. "Come inside and I'll make you a cup of hot tea and then we can talk."

Nella bit a fingernail. "*Denke.*"

When Adeline walked inside, her sister was nowhere in sight. "Where are you, Catherine?"

"I'm trying to sleep. Will you keep the noise level down?"

"Sorry, I was just wondering where you were."

"Well, I'm trying to sleep, so hush."

Adeline and Nella looked at each other.

Adeline said, "It seems her cold is making her cranky." After Adeline had put the teakettle on the stove, she sat down at the kitchen table with Nella. "What's happened?" Adeline asked as she placed her elbows on the table and rested her chin in her palms.

Nella shook her head. "It was terrible. He came out there to help my *onkel* and I could tell right away that he knew it was all a setup. He didn't stay long at all. He barely stayed long enough to do what he'd come to do before he left."

"What did you expect would happen?"

"Naturally, I thought he would stay longer and talk with me. Now I know he doesn't like me at all and all I've done is embarrass myself." She blinked back tears.

"Don't be upset. He could've had somewhere else that he had to be. He might have had other jobs waiting for him."

She shook her head. "*Nee,* I could tell. He was being really cold with me."

Adeline didn't know what to say to comfort her friend.

Nella continued, "And now Mary Lou will marry him and she doesn't deserve him at all because she's just horrible and … and… just mean sometimes."

"Nobody is perfect and she's not like that all the time," Adeline said.

"I suppose you think I'm mean now for saying all these things about Mary Lou, but she's never been nice to me."

Adeline thought more about Mary Lou and Joshua. "Do you really think Mary Lou and Joshua will marry?"

"I think they'll be married by the end of the year."

Mrs. Miller walked into the kitchen. "*Gut*, you've got the kettle on."

Right then, the kettle whistled.

"Would you like a cup of hot tea, *Mamm?*"

"I'll have a cup of *kaffe*, please, and I'll sit in the living room for a bit, and then we'll have to start preparing the evening meal."

From behind Nella, Mrs. Miller gave a look of disapproval before she walked out of the kitchen. After Adeline had made her friend and herself cups of hot tea, she took a cup of coffee out to her mother.

"How long will she be here for?" her mother whispered.

"Not long. She's feeling a bit better now." Adeline headed back to the kitchen. It was hard listening to her friend crying about the man that she was in love with, too.

"I don't know what I'm going to do," Nella said when Adeline sat back down in front of her.

"I wish I could help you, but I'm no expert in love since I've never had a boyfriend."

"Neither have I," said Nella. "Not a proper one. I've been on buggy rides, though and a date here and there. Joshua's the only man I've ever felt like this about."

"Just wait and see what happens. Do you think he knows you like him now?"

"*Jah*, and I'm so embarrassed. He said he doesn't like me that way. In fact, he wasn't happy about the whole thing. I've ruined everything now by having Hazel send him to my *onkel's*. You should've stopped me."

Adeline gulped. "I didn't want to ask Hazel, if you remember. There's something else I have to tell you."

"What?"

"I ran into Jacob Fuller today and he told me off good for having Hazel send Joshua to your *onkel's*. I guess it's got around that it was a set-up."

"It just gets worse."

"For me too. They're blaming me for saying something to Hazel. Everyone wants to protect Hazel and now they're seeing me as some mean girl."

"I'm sorry, Adeline, I shouldn't have gotten you involved. Why didn't you tell me before about Jacob?"

"It only happened today and this is the first time I've seen you. Anyway, Hazel must've told Joshua what she thought about it and then one of them must've said something to Jacob." She sighed. "*Mamm* and I have just come back from visiting Hazel and her mother. Hazel and I sorted everything out. She isn't upset about it." Adeline knew that Joshua was now even further away from her than ever.

"I'm so embarrassed. I wish I'd never done it. He doesn't like me at all, and now he never will. It's just plain humiliating." Nella heaved a sigh.

Adeline had to agree with her, and silently added that now Joshua was also mad at her.

She lifted the hot tea to her lips. It seemed everyone had problems. Hazel had problems with her mother, Catherine was sick, Nella and Mary Lou had problems with love. Was there anyone who didn't have any problems?

CHAPTER 14

THE NEXT DAY was Sunday and it was the Fullers' turn to have the meeting at their house. Adeline sat down next to Nella on one of the several long wooden benches that had been moved into the house for the meeting. All the Fullers' furniture had been moved out early that morning and replaced with the long wooden church benches.

Adeline looked around the large living room where Joshua had been raised. The beamed ceiling was high and three large gas lamps hung low from the ceiling. Mrs. Fuller was bustling about in the kitchen with some of the other women. Adeline looked forward to the next Sunday meeting when Lucy would be back and she could sit with her. Today, Catherine was still sick and Adeline had traveled to the meeting alone with her parents.

"Did you know that Timothy Fuller has gone on *rumspringa?*" Nella asked.

"*Nee,* I didn't."

"*Jah,* he's gone."

"Oh."

"I'm glad Joshua didn't go," Nella said.

"None of the other Fuller boys went did they? I know Levi never went."

"I think you're right."

Both Adeline and Nella fell silent when Mary Lou walked into the house wearing a new dress, dark grape in color and her apron and white prayer *kapp* stood out in stark contrast. Mary Lou had never worn that shade before and that was how Adeline knew the dress had to be new.

Mary Lou smiled and waved at them and made her way to them. Adeline was more than a little surprised when she sat down on the other side of her. Adeline was stuck between Mary Lou and Nella. She knew the two girls didn't really get along and now she was stuck between the two of them, like a piece of ham in a sandwich.

Adeline turned and asked Mary Lou. "How have you been?"

"Good, and you?"

"Great."

Mary Lou leaned across Adeline and said hello to

Nella. Nella smiled and said hello back as though they didn't have a problem with one another whatsoever. Even though both girls were smiling, Adeline could feel the tension thick in the air.

Then Joshua, Jacob, Samuel and Benjamin came down the stairs. The three girls had a good view of them, as the stairs ended in the center of the living room. Adeline's gaze was solely fixed on Joshua as the four Fuller boys shook hands with the other men as they made their way through the living room. Without even looking at them, Adeline knew who the girls on either side of her were looking at Joshua too.

Casually, Joshua turned his head in their direction and smiled. The brothers sat down on the men's side of the room, and pretty soon all the benches were full. The meeting began as soon as one of the deacons stood and opened it in prayer.

The bishop then preached on preferring other people over oneself. Adeline felt as though God was talking directly to her. She should step back and allow her friends a chance with Joshua even though she liked him too. It was only fair, as Mary Lou and Nella were both older than she.

When the meeting was coming to a close, she saw someone else who seemed to be staring at Joshua. It was Becky Stoltzfus. Adeline was certain that Becky was looking at Joshua rather than any of his brothers.

JOSHUA WASN'T happy about Adeline being friends with Mary Lou and Nella. He hoped they weren't saying anything negative about him. He'd had awkward encounters with both of them, and he just couldn't let them think he was interested in them. He'd done the best he could to discourage them without hurting their feelings, so he might have no choice but to be blunt.

He turned around to look at Adeline and all he saw was Becky Stoltzfus. She was blocking his view of Adeline and smiling at him. The only thing he could do was give a tiny nod and turn back to face the front.

Joshua was pleased when the meeting was over, but not because he didn't enjoy it. He was miserable because the room was far too hot. His mother felt the cold more than other people and she had insisted on keeping the fire going throughout the meeting.

He made his way through people, who were forming groups and greeting each other, and stepped out onto the porch. Breathing in the fresh air, he looked up at the puffy clouds, glad to be out of the stuffy living room. The day was overcast and gray, and the humidity was high.

"Hello, Joshua," said a small voice from behind him.

His heart leaped and he hoped it was Adeline's voice. He knew it wasn't Mary Lou's and he was certain it wasn't Nella's. He turned to see Becky and quickly hid the disappointment on his face the best he could.

"Hello, Becky."

"I hear your *bruder* has gone on *rumspringa* at the same time as my *bruder.*"

"That's right and let's hope they can keep each other out of trouble," he joked.

"We can pray about it," she said with not a hint of a smile around her thin serious lips.

"I've got no worries about Timothy. He'll be okay."

"Does that mean you have worries about John?" she asked, stepping closer.

"*Nee,* not at all. I just know Timothy much better, that's all. I've got no worries about anyone."

"Have you heard anything from Levi and Lucy?"

"*Nee,* but I think they're due to return in a few days."

"And they'll be living here for a while?"

Joshua nodded. "Only for a few days, I've been told. They've rented a little house not far away."

"That's nice. I guess your *Mamm's* pleased that her oldest boys are married now."

He smiled, thinking about his recent conversation with his mother. She might be pleased that her two oldest boys were married, but she certainly didn't approve of their choices of wives. He slowly nodded. He loosened the shirt around his neck, suddenly feeling another wave of heat come over him.

"Have you ever thought about being married?" she asked.

"I have," he said, tugging harder at his collar as he nearly choked.

"Do you think you would ever be interested in a woman like me?"

He'd never felt more awkward in his whole life. "I don't think I'm ready yet."

Her face fell. "Oh. When you are ready I'd like you to consider me."

"Denke. That's very flattering." He was distracted by Adeline coming out of the house and was disappointed when he saw Mary Lou and Nella accompanied her.

Becky glanced around to see where he was looking. Then she looked back at him. "I know I'm not the prettiest girl in the community, but sometimes the plainest make the best *fraas."*

He opened his mouth to say something and then could think of no reply. He wasn't the type of man to be influenced by somebody's looks, but the more he thought about it, he realized in the back of his mind, it made a difference. When Becky stayed there staring at him intently, he knew he had to reply. "I appreciate you saying what you did. I know it couldn't have been an easy thing to do."

"I thought I should say something because I have nothing to lose." She shrugged her shoulders and then left him standing there on the porch.

He was glad she hadn't invited him for an evening meal with her family. He'd been certain she was going to ask that. Looking down at the crowd of people now milling in his yard, he searched for Adeline. He saw her helping herself to a cup of soda. Alone. Now was his chance.

CHAPTER 15

ADELINE HEAVED a sigh of relief when Nella and Mary Lou walked off to have a private talk with one another. She was glad they weren't involving her in any way and was certain they were talking to clear the air between them.

Then she glanced over at Joshua and saw him talking with Becky. It seemed every time she looked at him, he was talking to a different girl. Remembering the bishop's words, she did her best to ignore the pang of jealousy that tore through her, and headed to the refreshment table.

Just as she finished pouring herself a glass, she felt someone beside her. In her heart, she knew it was Joshua.

"*Guder mayrie,* Adeline."

She turned slightly and faced him. "Hi, Joshua."

Now was her chance to make amends. If Jacob knew about what happened with Nella, then he had to have been told by Joshua. "I've been wanting to speak to you about something."

His mouth twitched at the corners. "What's that?"

After she had swallowed hard, she continued, "I need to apologize to you about speaking to Hazel."

"*Ach,* that."

"*Jah.* I shouldn't have done it and I'm sorry now that I didn't. I mean, that I did—did it. That I didn't say no."

He smiled at her stumbling over her words. "It's just that it put Hazel in a very difficult position and she's new to our community."

Adeline couldn't bear being reprimanded again, and especially not by the man she loved. She just wanted to run away and hide somewhere. "I know that. We've since talked and everything is okay between us."

"Between who?"

"Between me and Hazel."

He frowned. "I didn't know the two of you had a problem with one another."

"*Nee* we didn't, we don't. I just didn't want there to be any misunderstandings between Hazel and myself."

"I only have one question about it."

"What's that?"

"Why did you do it? Do you think it's Nella that I like?"

"I ... I ..." she tried to speak and all she could do was

stutter. Why did the man make her so nervous? "I don't know," she finally managed to say.

"It's not Nella."

He would've only told her that if he liked her. He was about to say something else, but then his attention was taken by something behind her. "Here come your friends. Can we talk about this another time?"

She nodded, and then he was gone. She turned around to see Nella and Mary Lou walking toward her. They didn't look too happy to see Joshua striding off in the other direction.

"Where is he going so quickly, Adeline?" Nella asked.

"What did you say to him?" Mary Lou added.

They'd both ruined what could've been a very special moment. "I barely said two words to him," Adeline said.

Suddenly, Mary Lou announced, "I'm going to help Mrs. Fuller with the food, okay?"

Before they could say anything, Mary Lou was charging toward the house.

Nella's mouth fell open. "Mary Lou wasn't even on the roster for today."

Adeline nodded. "Mrs. Fuller will like that."

"And that's the only reason she'd be doing it. When has Mary Lou ever helped with anything when she doesn't have to?"

Adeline shrugged her shoulders. "I don't know."

"Maybe I should go too. They might need more help today."

"*Nee*, that would be far too obvious if you help too. Mrs. Fuller would know something's up."

"You're right. If only I had thought of it first," Nella said.

"Do you want a soda?"

"*Nee*. I'm not thirsty."

Both girls moved away from the refreshments table when more people came over.

"Did you have a talk with Mary Lou?" Adeline asked.

"We had a really good talk."

"And?"

"Nothing was resolved, not really. The thing is that she likes Joshua and I love Joshua so I don't know what's gonna happen now. We're probably not the only ones who like him too."

Adeline nodded, thinking of herself and also Becky. "That's more than likely true."

"I wish he'd choose someone soon, and I hope it's me. Otherwise, I don't know what I'll do."

"You'll wait for *Gott* to send the man He's chosen for you, that's what."

It was Monday afternoon, and when the Fuller boys

arrived home from work they found that Levi and Lucy were back.

"I've been waiting for you to get back."

"You missed me?"

"A little. I figure a group of us will help you move in on Saturday and after that we'll have a get together with the young people."

"I don't know. We're a bit tired after all the traveling."

Joshua hoped he could change his mind. "It'll be done in no time at all and then we can all relax afterward."

"I'll ask Lucy." He chuckled. "Is there a reason why you want to do this so bad?"

"*Jah,* there is, but I can't tell you."

"Fair enough. I think I can guess."

"Well, keep the answer to yourself. Let me know what Lucy says. If she says no, I'll have to think something else up."

"If it means that much to you, I'll talk Lucy into it and at least it will mean that we'll get some help moving in."

"Exactly. *Denke* for that."

ON MONDAY AFTERNOON, Adeline and her mother were preparing the evening meal when they heard a horse and buggy outside their house.

Then they heard Catherine squeal from the living room, "It's Lucy!"

Their mother raced to the kitchen window and looked out. "She's alone. Levi isn't with her."

Adeline and Catherine both raced outside to see her, anxious to hear all the stories of her travels around the different communities. Lucy jumped down from the buggy and the three sisters hugged.

"Where's Levi?" Catherine asked.

"He's home. He's really tired, so he stayed at his parents' house. I couldn't stay. I had to come and see you all." Levi and Lucy were staying at the Fullers' house while they got their small rental home ready to move into.

Their mother appeared on the porch and called out, "Are you staying for dinner?"

"I don't think so, *nee*. I think the Fullers expect me to have dinner over there tonight since I'm staying there now."

Their mother nodded. "I suppose that makes sense since you're one of them now. Come in and tell us all your news."

Because she still wasn't feeling that well, Catherine got to sit at the table with Lucy while Mrs. Miller and Adeline continued preparing the evening meal.

"What's it like to be married?" Catherine asked.

"*Wunderbaar.* I feel safe and protected." Lucy giggled. "I love being married."

"Didn't you feel like that before—safe and protected?" their mother asked looking down her nose as she rolled out the pastry for the apple pie.

"*Jah,* but it's different. I was part of this family when I was a child and now that I'm grown, I'll have my own family and be the *mudder.* I can't wait."

"It'll happen soon enough," their mother said.

"I hope so, then I'll have dozens of nieces running around," Catherine said.

"Not dozens," Adeline said, "and what about nephews?"

"*Nee,* I just want Lucy to have girls." Catherine giggled.

Mrs. Miller stopped rolling out the pastry. "How long will you be staying with Levi's family?"

"Less than a week probably. We just need help to move all the furniture over from their barn and then bring my hope chest and everything from here."

"We'll help," Catherine said.

Mrs. Miller shook the wooden rolling pin at her youngest daughter. "You won't be doing anything for a while. Not with the bad wheeze you've got."

"I'm fine."

"You're sick?" Lucy asked Catherine.

"*Jah,* she's had a bad cold and now she's got a wheeze in her chest."

Catherine pulled a face. "I don't like the word 'wheeze.'"

"Well, that's what it is."

"It's more of a squeak. I might need oiling," Catherine joked.

"No you don't, not with all of the butter you eat," laughed Adeline, and she was quickly joined by her mother and sisters.

"All the same, you won't be going anywhere for a while. The Fullers have enough men in the family to help do all that."

Catherine slumped low in her chair. "I feel like a prisoner."

"No prisoner eats as much as you do," Adeline said.

"I've not finished growing yet. I need to eat a lot."

Lucy smiled. "I can see nothing's changed around here since I've been gone."

CHAPTER 16

DURING DINNER, Joshua told his brothers about the get-together that Levi had agreed to.

"I love a good party," Benjamin said.

"A party? Aren't you having everyone there to do work, Levi? A working bee?" Mrs. Fuller asked.

"I thought it was a party," Benjamin said.

"You would think it was a party," Jacob said. "You don't take anything seriously."

"I'll do work as well, and then I won't say no to a 'get-together'—if that's what you'd like to call it." Benjamin smiled at Joshua.

Lucy put her hand to her mouth and giggled at Benjamin, only to get half a scowl from Mrs. Fuller.

"It would be a *gut* idea because you need a few men to move all your furniture," Mrs. Fuller said.

"That'll only take half a day," Levi said.

"Exactly, and what will we do with the rest of the day?" Benjamin asked. "Have a party. A house-warming party."

Mrs. Fuller shook her head in despair at her youngest son, and then stared into her beef and cabbage stew.

Levi turned to Lucy, who was sitting right beside him. "What do you think?"

"I like the idea. And we should do it on Saturday."

"Perfect," Joshua said. "We won't work at the shop this Saturday. We've caught up on all our orders and we've got that big hotel job wrapped up."

Mr. Fuller leaned forward and spoke in his usual slow and calculated way. "That's only if nothing urgent crops up before then."

"Jah, if nothing urgent turns up before that," Joshua said. This was something he would be able to invite Adeline to. She would most likely have turned up anyway because Lucy was her sister, but if he asked her personally that would give her a hint of how he felt about her. After that, he wouldn't push things. Love should grow in its own time.

THE VERY NEXT day after work, Joshua summoned up as much courage as he could and drove his buggy to the Millers' house to ask Adeline to accompany him on

Saturday. He got down from his buggy, walked quickly to the door and knocked on it. Mrs. Miller opened the door and stared at him.

"Hello, Mrs. Miller. Could I speak with Adeline? I'll only be a moment."

"She's not home. I'm sorry, Joshua."

Embarrassed, he hung his head.

"Is anything wrong?" she asked.

"*Nee,* I just wanted to talk with her, that's all."

"Oh." And then the penny seemed to drop. "Oh." Mrs. Miller smiled. "She's at Hazel's *haus.*"

"Hazel?"

"*Jah.*"

"I just happened to be heading there now." He hadn't been going anywhere until he heard Adeline was there.

"*Gut.*"

He gave her a smile and she gave him a nod as though she approved of him being fond of her daughter. At least, that was what he hoped it meant.

As he walked to the buggy, he heard the front door close. Then when he climbed in the buggy, he looked back at the house and saw a curtain move from the window in one of the upstairs rooms. He could see Adeline's younger sister staring at him. He drove away laughing to himself. Catherine couldn't have known that he could see her so plainly through the curtain.

If only he had known Adeline was at Hazel's then it

wouldn't have appeared so odd. He could've arrived there as though he was going to talk to Isaac. Then he reminded himself that he'd decided to give her a hint of his feelings. "She'll surely know I like her when she learns I called at her *haus*," he said aloud to himself. All the way there, he prepared himself to be let down. Adeline might not like him at all.

HAZEL HAD BEEN on Adeline's mind, and Adeline had decided to visit her hoping that things had gotten better for both Hazel and her mother.

"How's your *mudder* coping with everything?"

"She's better. Much better since your *mudder's* visit."

"Good. *Mamm* wanted to come this evening, but she said she wasn't feeling the best, so she might come tomorrow during the day and visit your *mudder*."

"That would be really good if she could. *Mamm's* had such a hard time, but she's starting to feel like this is her home."

"She is?"

"*Jah*. It was a quick turnaround. Her sister said she'd visit soon, so that made her happy. I'm not certain if she's just putting on a brave face, but I'm not complaining. I used to complain. I used to ask, 'why me?' all the time. 'Why did I have to be the one to have a *vadder* like that?'"

Adeline nodded in sympathy and wondered how she'd feel if she were in that situation.

"All I wanted was a happy family like my friends had. *Mamm* could've married a different man."

Adeline pointed out, "Then you might not be here, if she'd married a different man."

"I guess that's true."

"Then who would Isaac have married?" Adeline asked and then remembered Mary Lou whom he'd very nearly married.

"I can think of a girl he would've married," Hazel said.

"Ach nee, don't even say that."

Hazel smiled. "I'm happy now, and I just want my *mudder* to be the same."

"She will be, when she holds your *boppli* in her arms."

Hazel nodded. "I hope so."

WHEN JOSHUA TURNED off the road to go to Hazel and Isaac's house, a buggy was heading toward him. It was Adeline's buggy heading away from the house. He'd nearly missed her.

He moved his buggy off the road and pulled up his horse. When she came closer, she smiled at him and waved.

"Wait, Adeline."

She stopped the buggy. "Hello, Joshua."

His heart pumped hard against his chest. She looked lovely in the semi-darkness with her face framed by the light tendrils of hair that had escaped her prayer *kapp.* "Hello. I just called at your *haus.* I wanted to speak to you. Your *mudder* said you were here." She looked at him and didn't speak. "Remember how I told you that I'd ask you somewhere?"

"Jah."

"This Saturday coming, Levi and Lucy are having people help them move their furniture in and then they're having a ..." he remembered Benjamin's words about having a party, but didn't want to say that. "They're having a meal afterward. Would you like to come—with me?"

"Oh, I thought you'd still be mad with me because of Hazel and ..."

"I'm not mad with you. Why would you think that?"

"Because of what Jacob said."

Joshua frowned. "When did you see Jacob?"

"At the markets on Saturday."

"He never mentioned he saw you. What did he say?" Joshua hoped that Jacob hadn't ruined everything for him with Adeline.

"I thought you would've known. I thought I knew I'd talked to him."

Joshua's eyebrows rose. *"Nee.* He didn't upset you, did he?"

She shook her head, but Joshua could tell his brother had upset her. "I'm sorry. It wasn't his place to say anything."

"When you and I spoke recently I thought you knew that he talked to me. Anyway, the whole thing was my fault. I shouldn't have gotten involved."

"If you don't mind me asking, why did you?"

She shrugged. "If a friend asks for help, it's hard to say no."

"I know what you mean. I just didn't like to have things arranged without knowing about it. Will you come to Lucy's and Levi's with me?"

She nodded. *"Jah* I will."

"Can I collect you and take you home?"

She didn't want to hurt anyone's feelings. "That might be a bit difficult. I can see you there."

He was disappointed, but he was pretty sure he knew why she wouldn't be seen traveling in the buggy with him. It must've been that she didn't want to upset her friend.

WHEN ADELINE GOT HOME, the first thing she did was pour her heart out to her younger sister. She told her everything. "I don't know what to do, Catherine."

"From what you've told me, it's clear that he likes you. He doesn't like Nella or Mary Lou, and anyway, who would like Mary Lou?"

"Catherine! That's a dreadful thing to say."

"Jah, I know. I've got to stop being so mean. I'm working on it."

"You really think he likes me?" Adeline asked.

"Jah. He wanted to collect you on Saturday, didn't he?"

Adeline nodded.

"See? He didn't ask anyone else."

"Nee, he didn't."

Catherine shook her head. "You should've agreed to go with him."

"How could I? Nella's been crying over him and Mary Lou's made no secret about liking him. How can I hurt my friends like that?"

"I would. I would if I liked someone and he liked me. Joshua doesn't like them, so you're not hurting them, not really. They can find other men."

"I don't like to see people upset."

"What about you?"

Adeline tipped her head to the side. "What do you mean?"

"You're a person too, and don't you deserve to be with the man you want?"

"I guess so. I hadn't thought of things in that way. You've got a special way of seeing things."

"Go to his place right now and say you've changed your mind and he can pick you up."

Adeline giggled. *"Nee,* I can't do that. The moment's gone. Anyway, I have to forget about him."

"Nee, you don't." Catherine grunted. "Why are you so hopeless?"

"I'm not, I'm just considering other people's feelings."

"I'll be well enough to go on Saturday. I'll go with you."

"It depends what *Mamm* says."

"I'll be well enough." Catherine's voice rose.

"You're not going to do something stupid, are you?"

Catherine shook her head. "Of course I won't."

THAT NIGHT, Joshua closed himself in his room right after dinner. Why was it that the only girl he liked didn't openly like him back? At times, he was certain she liked him, but then she wouldn't accept his invitation to travel in his buggy. Did she have concerns for her friends, was that all it was? He had to single her out on Saturday and get to the bottom of things.

JOSHUA and the men worked on all the jobs that needed

to be done on Levi's leased house. It was a small house on two fenced acres with a large barn. When most of the work was done, more people arrived. Adeline had been there the whole time, helping Lucy unpack boxes inside the house.

Nella kept away from him, but as soon as Mary Lou arrived she walked up to him. He'd just finished helping to organize the barn.

"I didn't know you'd be here," she said to him as though nothing had happened in the past.

"Levi's my *bruder,* so I couldn't really get out of it."

Mary Lou giggled. "I guess not."

"Did you just get here?"

"I tried to come earlier, I mean, I would've, but I was called into work this morning. I don't like to turn them down when they ask me to come in. Someone was sick."

Loud giggling caught their attention and they both turned to look at the group of girls.

"Looks like the party's already starting."

She giggled again. "Can I bring you a soda, or anything else?"

"Nee. I need to get cleaned up." He dusted off his hands. "I'll catch up with you later." After he gave her a smile, he walked away. Before he reached the house, Becky Stoltzfus called out to him.

He turned and waited for her to catch up to him. "Hi, Joshua."

"Hello, Becky."

"Have you heard from your *bruder?*"

"You mean Timothy?"

"Jah."

"Nee. Is he okay?"

"He seems to be. He's got a place to lease with John, and did you know they're buying a car together?"

"Nee, I didn't."

She stepped closer to him. "What do you think about that?"

"What part of it?"

"I just said that your *bruder* and John are going to buy a car together."

"I heard you." It was always awkward talking with Becky. Conversations never flowed with her. "That sounds like a good plan."

"Don't you think it means they'll be out of the community for longer if they're buying cars?"

"I guess they need to travel, so it makes sense to buy one and pool their resources. It's practical."

"Cars can be dangerous."

"So can buggies. Anything has a chance of being dangerous. I wouldn't worry. They're in *Gott's* hands."

"But are they, if they're on *rumspringa?* They're not saved until they're baptized and neither of them has been."

He didn't want to stand there talking about hypothetical things. No one really knew where someone ended up if they died on their *rumspringa* with the intention of returning to the community. He didn't want to be rude to Becky, but neither did he want to talk to her for the sake of talking. The only woman he wanted to talk to was Adeline. "*Gott* has it in hand. He knows the beginning from the end."

"I know, but—"

Mary Lou interrupted, "Becky, will you excuse me for a moment? I need to speak to Joshua in private for a moment."

Joshua had never been so pleased to see Mary Lou. He stared at Becky waiting for her to reply. It took a while, but she eventually gave a reluctant nod and stepped back. Mary Lou grabbed the edge of his sleeve and pulled him away a few paces.

He frowned at her. "What is it?"

"I've been watching you and I know what's going on with you."

"What do you mean?"

"You're in love with Adeline."

He couldn't believe his ears. Should he deny it? He couldn't do that because what she said was true. "I don't know what you want me to say."

"There's nothing to say. Why couldn't you have just been honest with me in the first place rather than leading me on like you did?"

He studied her face to see if she might be joking. She wasn't. "I never led you on, Mary Lou."

She put her hands on her hips and tipped back her chin. "You did."

"Well, I surely didn't intend to, and if I did, I'm sorry."

"Is that all you've got to say?"

"Jah. There's nothing else I can say."

"And you admit that you're in love with Adeline Miller?" Her voice rose as though she deliberately wanted everyone to hear.

"That's my personal business, Mary Lou, and I would appreciate it if you kept your voice down and I would further appreciate it if you kindly don't discuss me with anyone else."

"I'll tell Adeline the kind of man that you are." She shot him a glare and stomped away.

His heart was racing. He didn't like arguments and neither did he like upsetting people. Now all eyes were on him and he needed to get away somewhere by himself.

As he was looking for a quiet spot by the barn, thinking perhaps of even ducking behind it, Benjamin came toward him. "I saw you talking to Mary Lou just now. It seems you upset her."

"I didn't."

"Looks like it to me. Was it a lover's tiff?"

"Cut it out, Benjamin. You know things aren't like that with me and her."

"Well, what do you want things to be like with her?"

He pulled a face. "Nothing. Absolutely nothing."

"Who do you like then?" Benjamin asked.

"Not Mary Lou."

"Why not?"

He glared at his brother, wanting him to stop antagonizing him.

"What's wrong?" Benjamin asked.

"Nothing's wrong. Just stop talking to me about Mary Lou."

"Okay. I was just off to talk to Adeline anyway."

Joshua jumped in front of his brother. "You're going to what?"

"Talk to Adeline. She's by herself in the kitchen."

"I'll talk to her. There's no need for you to do it. Weren't you going to ask every girl out and none of them were going to say no to you, or something? No wait, that was Jacob."

"Yeah, it sounds like something Jacob would say. I'm totally opposite to him."

"Good." Joshua saw Jacob coming toward them. "I'll go talk to Adeline."

"What's stopping you?" Benjamin raised his eyebrows, and then Joshua knew that his brother might be the youngest in the family, but Benjamin was smart enough to figure out that he liked Adeline. Or perhaps he'd overheard Mary Lou? It wouldn't have been hard since she had all but yelled it out.

"What's going on with you two?" Jacob asked.

Benjamin took a step back to allow Jacob room to join the conversation. "We're talking about women."

Jacob laughed. "And what would you know about women, Benjamin?"

"Enough. And if you know so much, why aren't you married?" Benjamin asked Jacob.

"Jah, Jacob?" Joshua crossed his arms and stared at Jacob, glad the attention was off him for a change.

"Finding the right woman. I told you all this, Joshua. Why are you so jumpy all of a sudden?" Jacob looked back at the house. Adeline could be seen through the kitchen window. "Haven't you asked Adeline out yet?"

He sighed. Now it seemed everyone knew he liked Adeline. "I'm still thinking about it. I'm worried that she's too young, like you kindly keep reminding me."

"Is she?" Benjamin smiled.

"I don't think so. Not for me, but maybe for you," Jacob said.

"You told me you wouldn't compete with me."

"Jah, well, depends how long you take, though."

"And you were talking like you didn't like her, or thought she wasn't sweet. You said that just the other day."

Jacob chuckled. "I can handle a girl who's not that sweet and if you think Adeline's perfect you're setting yourself up for a fall."

"You're wrong about her. Anyway, I need to take my time. Everything needs to be perfect. I don't want to scare her away by making a move too early." Joshua's ego was still bruised that she'd refused his offer to pick her up. He was too embarrassed to tell his brothers that.

"If you ask me, you should do something about it," Benjamin said.

"*Jah*. She's there alone in the kitchen right now. This is a perfect time to say something to her," Jacob added.

"*Nee*, I can't. I made a small move and things didn't go how I expected."

"You need to learn a thing or two about women—" Benjamin started saying.

"I need to?" Joshua asked thinking that was funny coming from the baby of the family.

"*Jah*. If you're going to hold such a high standard that someone can't make one mistake you're never going to marry anyone."

Joshua took off his hat and ran a hand through his hair.

"I guess the kid's right. What are you waiting for?" Jacob asked.

"Okay. I'll do it." Joshua put his hat back on and strode toward the house. When he was inside, he made his way to the kitchen and peeped in. "Adeline."

She turned around. "Joshua."

He closed the distance between them. "I'm sorry for everything I said to you before, the other day."

"You don't have to be, you were right. I should've

never let myself get into that position. It was uncomfortable but I thought I couldn't say no. I felt I had to do it."

"Why?"

"I was trying to help a friend, and now I think no one likes me anymore. Everyone seems upset with me."

"I'm not."

The corners of her lips turned up slightly. "You were before."

"Well, I'm not now."

"Good."

"Can I get you something? Maybe some soda?" There was a table with food and drinks set up outside the house.

"That would be nice."

"What are you doing in here alone?"

"I'm cleaning up the kitchen while Lucy's supervising where things should be stored in the barn."

"Come and walk with me. If I leave you alone, someone might talk to you and I'll lose my place by your side."

She giggled.

He laughed. "I mean it. Some of these men are ruthless, my *bruders* included."

"I'll remember that, but you must remember that my *schweschder* married your *bruder*, so you have to watch what you say about your *brieder*."

"I will. *Denke* for the reminder."

They both walked toward the table where the drinks were. Benjamin and Samuel were hanging colored lanterns in nearby tree branches, ready for when the sun went down. Jacob was nowhere to be seen and neither were Mary Lou, Becky, or Nella. Joshua carefully poured Adeline a glass of orange soda and then poured one for himself. When someone started hammering loudly on something, Joshua said, "Let's walk over that way so we can hear ourselves speak."

"Okay."

ADELINE'S INSIDES felt like a light had been turned on; she was glowing. She was nervous talking to him and she hoped he liked her. She knew he'd been out with a few girls but had never had a long-term girlfriend. Most of the girls in her group of friends were in love with either Joshua or his next-younger brother, Jacob.

"Can I drive you home tonight? I know you've already said no to my bringing you here, but I'm hoping you'll change your mind about me driving you home."

Now she knew for certain he liked her. She'd refused his first offer, and now he'd gotten his courage up and asked again, so she knew his interest in her was strong. For once she thought about herself, and took her younger sister's advice. She'd stepped aside for long enough, until she was certain that he didn't like Mary Lou or Nella. She'd done the right thing as far as she could. *"Jah. Dat* drove me here and that would save Lucy from taking me home."

He smiled at her and his eyes twinkled. "I wasn't thinking of the practical aspects."

She looked down and knew she was blushing.

"And maybe, we could do something sometime soon, just the two of us?"

Looking back up at him, she asked, "Like what?"

"Maybe I'll surprise you. What do you think about that?"

Adeline couldn't keep the smile from her face. "I'd like that."

"Me too. Shall I collect you on Saturday morning? Would you like to spend the day with me?"

She nodded, suddenly too choked up to speak. All she wanted to do was jump up and down and holler. She couldn't wait to get home and tell Catherine. Catherine had been determined to go to Lucy's, but their mother still wasn't convinced she was well enough to go anywhere without risking a relapse.

For the next few hours, Joshua barely left her side and she could feel Nella and Mary Lou glaring at her as they stood together talking. Adeline didn't look at them. They'd each had their chance with Joshua, and she'd taken a backseat to them for long enough.

"Are you ready to go home now?" Joshua asked her.

If they left now, they would be among the first to leave. "Okay, I'll just say goodbye to Lucy.

"Okay."

As Adeline made her way through the crowd to find Lucy, she was confronted by Nella.

"What's going on with you and Joshua?"

"He's driving me home."

"So, you like him?"

"I've liked him for a long time. Before you liked him."

"Why didn't you tell me?"

Adeline swallowed hard. "I didn't like to because you liked him so much."

Nella nodded. "You should've said something."

"Maybe I should've, but I didn't know what to do."

"Denke for being a good friend to me, Adeline." Nella stepped in to give her a hug.

Adeline nodded, happy that Nella was pleased for her. She doubted she'd get a similar response from Mary Lou. "I'm going home now."

"I'll be waiting to hear what happens, and you must tell me everything."

Adeline giggled. "Okay."

When she spotted Lucy, she was shocked to see her talking with Mary Lou. She approached them both. "Good night. I'm going now."

"Oh, I'll find Levi to take you home. He's also taking a few other people home."

"*Nee*, Lucy, it's fine."

"How are you getting home?" Mary Lou asked.

"Joshua is taking me home."

Mary Lou frowned. "Is that right?"

"*Jah.* Goodnight." Adeline leaned in and hugged both girls in turn and then turned to go back to Joshua. It had worked out well that Mary Lou had found out like that, when she was standing there with Lucy.

As she walked back to Joshua, she saw his face light up.

"Ready?"

"*Jah.*"

"Let's go."

On the drive home, Joshua asked, "Would you like to come to a family dinner on Friday night? Lucy and Levi will be there too."

"I'd love to come. Should I come early to help your *mudder?* It sounds like there'll be a fair few people to cook for."

"I could ask. She's a little possessive of her kitchen."

"Oh, well, maybe don't ask her."

"*Nee,* I'll ask. She'll appreciate the gesture. I'm happy you agreed for me to drive you home."

"Me too."

"I don't want there to be any misunderstanding between us." He glanced over at her. "The truth is I've liked you for a while and I didn't say anything, because

I didn't know if you'd think I was too old or too …
something."

"I don't think you're too old or too … anything," she
said with a cheeky grin, "and you know why I couldn't
let you know how I felt."

"Jah. I understand." When he pulled up at her house,
he said, "I had a lovely night."

"Me too. *Denke* for arranging it."

"I'll see you on Friday night."

"What time? It'll have to be early if I'm helping your
mudder."

"Make it five. I'll collect you at five."

Adeline knew from the time he'd chosen that she
wouldn't be helping Mrs. Fuller in the kitchen.

As though reading her mind, he said, *"Mamm* will
say you're a guest and shouldn't help. But I'll still tell
her you offered."

"Okay." She gave a little giggle. Then she stepped
down from the buggy. *"Gut nacht,* Joshua."

"Gut nacht."

She hurried to the darkened house while listening
to him turning his horse and buggy back around to
face the road. When she opened the front door, she saw
a small light on just near the fireplace. Beside it was
Catherine, asleep. Adeline knew she'd fallen asleep
waiting for her.

"Wake up," Adeline said in her ear.

Catherine started moving, and then opened her eyes. "You're home."

"Jah, and guess who brought me home?"

She straightened up and opened her eyes wide. "Joshua?"

"Jah."

"Sit down and tell me everything and don't leave anything out."

Adeline sat next to her and did just that.

AS JOSHUA DROVE home along the moonlit street, he wondered how his mother would react to the news that Adeline Miller would be joining them for the Friday night family dinner. This was the first girl he'd ever invited home and his mother would know he was interested in her. He bit his lip, remembering the promise to his mother that he'd marry a girl that would be just like a *dochder* to her. His mother wasn't happy with Hazel or Lucy, and Lucy and Adeline were sisters. It was a bad start. He didn't want to disappoint his mother, so he knew he'd have to break the news gently.

CHAPTER 17

I<small>T WAS</small> the next Monday evening after work that Joshua decided his mother should know about Adeline coming to dinner on Friday night. It was important that the dinner go well because Adeline had also agreed to spend the whole of Saturday with him and he didn't want anything to ruin that.

He figured on Saturday he'd take her for a long buggy ride along the winding back roads and visit some of the historic covered bridges. Then, for lunch, a picnic by the river. He'd get Hazel to help him pack a nice lunch. She'd know where to get all the food and what he should take. Hazel and Adeline got along well, so surely Hazel would be happy to help.

As usual at this time of day, his mother was in the kitchen busily humming as she flitted from one side of the room to the other.

"Mamm, have you got a moment?"

She glanced at him. "Is anything wrong? You're not ill, are you?"

"Nee, not at all. I just want to have a word with you."

"Do I have to sit down or can I keep cooking?"

"You can keep cooking." He thought she might take the news better that way. "I invited someone to dinner on Friday night."

The saucepan she'd been holding landed heavily on top of the stove, and she swung around to look at him. "Who?"

"Adeline Miller."

Her mouth fell open and her face immediately lost all its color. "Who?" she asked in a quiet voice as though she hoped she had heard wrong.

"Adeline, Lucy's *schweschder.*"

She headed for the table, pulled out a chair, and then sat heavily. "You're inviting Adeline Miller?"

He sat down next to her. "That's right, *Mamm.*"

She looked into his face. "Do you like her?"

"Very much. I drove her home Saturday night from Levi's new *haus.*"

"Oh. Hmm."

"I know what you're thinking."

"Do you?"

"Jah, you said you wanted me to marry a girl you could think of as your *dochder,* and I know you don't think..."

"Never mind what I said a few days ago. Sometimes I'm a selfish woman."

Joshua gasped. "Nee, you're not."

"I am. I can't choose who you marry. Now if I could choose, I'd choose Mary Lou. I didn't like her at first and then she grew on me over time."

He couldn't believe his ears. "Really?"

"The point I'm trying to make is that you should choose someone who'll make you happy. Someone who's a hardworking girl, unselfish, and kind. And someone who'll be a *gut mudder* and, if you think that girl is Adeline, then you should marry her."

He stared at his mother, wondering whether she was doing some kind of reverse psychology thing on him. He'd never mentioned marriage, Adeline was only coming to dinner, but it was marriage he had in his heart. He wanted to marry Adeline, but he didn't want to rush her, considering her young age.

"*Denke* for understanding, *Mamm.* I was a little afraid to tell you."

"When I said that to you the other day, I regretted it when I played over the words in my head later that night. I just didn't get the chance to tell you to disregard my silliness."

"Well, if I do end up marrying Adeline, I hope you'll feel she's a *dochder* to you—the *dochder* you always wanted and never had."

She chuckled. "That's the one thing I want, but I might have to wait for that. Maybe it'll be Jacob's *fraa*."

Joshua was a little disappointed that she'd added that last bit. He had thought he was finally getting through to her. "Adeline offered to come early to help you cook."

"*Nee*, I like to be the only one in the kitchen. I'm used to it by now, what with raising all boys, and I like things done just so."

"It was nice of her to ask, though. Don't you think so?" Joshua asked, hoping his mother might say something nice about Adeline.

"*Jah*, it was. Now, I'd better get a move on with this dinner."

CHAPTER 18

ON FRIDAY AFTERNOON, Adeline anxiously awaited Joshua's arrival to collect her.

"Stop pacing," her mother said. "He'll be here soon enough."

"Yeah, it's not even five yet. It's ten minutes before."

"I know, but did he mean he'd collect me at five, or should we arrive at his parents' *haus* at five?"

"Relax and sit down," Catherine said. "You'll use up all your energy and you need to save it so you'll impress Mrs. Fuller with some sparkling conversation and witty repartee."

Adeline scoffed. "I don't think I'll have much of that happening. I figure it's best to keep quiet, so I don't keep putting my foot in my mouth."

From the couch, her mother turned to her. "You don't need to impress anybody, Adeline, just be yourself. You're a sweet young woman. You can't go wrong if you just be yourself."

"*Denke, Mamm.*" Adeline put her fingertips to her forehead. It was burning. "I think I'm coming down with something."

"*Nee* you're not," Catherine snapped. "You're just nervous, so your hands have gone cold. Pull yourself together. It's only a dinner for crying out loud."

"Stop getting yourself worked up," her mother said.

Adeline wanted to get away from both of them telling her what to do and how to behave. But if she went outside, it would look like she was waiting for Joshua ... which she was, but she didn't want to appear too anxious.

"I'll get a drink of water." She headed to the kitchen and as she took a swallow of water, she heard a buggy. It could only be either her father coming home from work or Joshua. Looking out the kitchen window, she saw Joshua's buggy.

Catherine ran into the kitchen. "He's here."

"I know. I saw."

"I'll wait up."

"*Denke.*" She hugged Catherine and then hugged her mother who was now standing behind Catherine.

Before she walked outside, she grabbed her black shawl from behind the door. It wasn't cold, but she found comfort in her soft shawl. When she opened the door, Joshua was halfway from his buggy to the house.

"Hello, Adeline. You look lovely."

"Denke."

"Are you ready?"

"Jah."

"Let's go."

They climbed into the buggy and Adeline pulled the shawl to her stomach. She had no idea how she was going to eat. Her tummy was churning.

As the horse pulled the buggy back out to the road, Joshua glanced over at her. "Are you cold?"

"Nee." She giggled. "I guess I'm a little nervous. This is my 'security shawl.'"

"Don't be nervous. I'll be there, and Lucy will be there too."

She nodded feeling a little better.

"And don't worry about my *mudder.* She looks fierce, but she's not. She's soft."

"Is she?"

"Jah."

Adeline wasn't so sure of that.

"I might be getting carried away and looking too far into the future, but both of us can't worry what people think about us being together."

"We're together?" Did he mean they were dating —courting?

"That's what I'd like, if that's what you want too." He stared at her waiting for an answer.

She allowed herself to relax a little. "I do, and you're

right about not being concerned about other people. My *schweschder* says I've done that too much."

"Catherine?"

"Jah."

"She's quite wise for a young girl, I'd say. Is she still ill? I haven't seen her lately."

"She's getting better, but *Mamm's* being a bit over-protective and won't let her out of the *haus."*

"Ah, *mudders.* What would we do without them?"

Adeline laughed. "They mean well. I've just realized you've got all boys in your family and I've got all girls."

"That's right. My *mudder* always wanted a girl, but it wasn't to be. What about your *mudder?"*

"She's never really said. I think she wanted more *kinner* than three, but it never happened."

Three children were a small number to have for an Amish family.

"Just relax tonight and try to enjoy yourself. We'll do something nice tomorrow by ourselves. I've probably thrown you in the deep end, but I wanted to see you sooner than Saturday. That was probably selfish of me, it was just a night extra I would have had to wait."

"I'm pleased. I wanted to see you before tomorrow as well."

Joshua turned to her and gave her a beaming smile and all her worries left her.

The worry returned, however, when they got to the

house and saw his mother standing on the porch with her arms folded.

"Looks like something's wrong," he said.

"Maybe she's changed her mind about me coming."

"*Nee.* It can't be that."

He got out of the buggy and hurried toward his mother with Adeline following close behind. "What is it, *Mamm?*"

"It's Timothy. He's crashed his car. He's not harmed, but he's shaken and refusing to come home, and the police are involved."

"How did you find out?"

"The police came here because he had this address on his license. The police said he had an accident and didn't stop."

"Where's everyone else?"

"Your *vadder* wants to keep out of it and let him settle his own problems. He said that's the path he chose. Samuel and the other boys are still at work finishing something off, and Levi and Isaac are still helping people with their Friday night jobs."

"They're still there?"

"You left them shorthanded when you left early to get Adeline. Isaac called to tell me they'd be late." His mother looked at Adeline and looked back at Joshua. "We'll have to cancel dinner."

"Hello, Mrs. Fuller. I'm sorry for your troubles."

"Hello, Adeline. *Denke,* it will all work out, I'm sure."

Joshua turned to Adeline. "Would you mind very much staying here until I get back? You can have dinner with my folks while I sort Timothy out." He swung back to his mother. "Will that be okay, *Mamm?*"

"*Jah*. I think Adeline and I have a lot we can talk about."

Adeline nodded when Joshua looked back at her.

"Good. Do you know where Timothy is, *Mamm?*"

"*Nee.* He's either at the police station or at … the place he and John live."

"I'll make a few calls." He looked at Adeline. "You go inside with *Mamm* and I'll see you later. Unless you'd like me to take you back home?"

"*Nee* I'll be fine here. If that's okay with you, Mrs. Fuller?"

"It is. *Denke,* Joshua. Also make some calls and cancel the family dinner. It'll only be the family who live here that eat here tonight. As well as Adeline."

CHAPTER 19

WHILE JOSHUA HURRIED to the phone in the barn, Adeline trudged up the front porch steps. He'd said he wouldn't leave her side all night and now she'd be having dinner with the other Fuller boys and Mr. and Mrs. Fuller. It wasn't the night she'd been hoping for.

"Come in the kitchen and talk to me, Adeline. The food is nearly finished."

"Okay, *denke*."

Once they were in the kitchen, Mrs. Fuller ordered her to sit down. Adeline sat at the long wooden table in the open dining area adjoining the large kitchen. Adeline's hands ran over the grain of the table.

"This is such a beautiful table. The wood is so lovely."

"My *vadder* made that table. It's solid Cherrywood."

"I love the color."

"Me too. He made it for my *mudder* when I was a young *maedel.*" Mrs. Fuller seemed pleased that she liked the table and she sat down with her. "I've got so many fond memories attached to this table. It's silly really. It's just a table, but it's as though it has a life of its own."

"My *Mamm's* like that with the clock *Dat* gave her for a wedding present. But a dreadful thing happened to it."

"What?"

"Oh, well, the thing is, *Mamm* still doesn't know, but one time when my younger *schweschder* was cleaning it, it slipped out of her hands. Well, the complete truth is that she was pretending to drop it. We often played around like that when we were dusting, and anyway, it so happened that she really dropped it."

"Why doesn't your *mudder* know?"

"She was out visiting at the time and we knew she'd be so upset if it was broken. She looks at it every day and smiles. *Dat* gave it to her on their wedding day and I think it brings back happy memories to her. Like this table does for you. It's cream-colored with tiny blue and pink flowers—"

"What happened?"

"*Ach, jah.* Well, we found some glue in the barn and carefully glued it back together. It wasn't broken at the front and the clock still worked. The glue set quickly and now you can only see a fine line." Adeline's fingertips flew to her mouth. Adeline and Catherine had never told anyone—they'd never dared to, not even Lucy, in case their mother found out. "You won't tell her, will you?"

"*Nee,* of course I won't. She'd be too upset, and besides, Catherine didn't break it on purpose."

"We shouldn't have been horsing around like that."

"You were only trying to pass the time in a joyful manner."

"I guess so. And *Mamm* winds it every day and because the living room is dark, she's never noticed."

"And let's hope she never will." Mrs. Fuller gave a little chuckle. "One day I might have time to tell you some of my memories around this table."

"I'd like that very much."

"Would you?" Mrs. Fuller seemed surprised.

"*Jah.*"

"*Denke.* For now, how about you help me with making the sauce for dinner?"

"I'd love to help."

FOR THE SAKE OF TIME, Joshua called a taxi and headed to the police station where Timothy and John were. He quickly unhitched the horse, rubbed him down, and returned him to the paddock while awaiting the taxi.

When he arrived at the station, Timothy and John were sitting on the stairs waiting for him. He paid the taxi fare and walked up to them, anxious to hear what had happened.

"It wasn't our fault," was the first thing Timothy said as he stood up.

John stood too. "Yeah, these guys were picking on us and trying to run us off the road and then I swerved and then they ran into a ditch. Then they called the cops on us."

"Did the police charge you with anything?"

"Nah, we're free to go. They said these guys had outstanding warrants against them, so now they're locked up."

"So, you've got no charges against you and no fines?"

"No," John said.

"Only the thing is ..."

"Our car's totaled."

"Jah. Now we've got no wheels."

Joshua shook his head. "We'll get a taxi, and then I'll take you back to your place before I head home."

"How about a loan?" Timothy asked. "So we can buy another car."

Joshua rubbed his neck. He had the money, but what if the second car ended up the same as the first one? Was he teaching them a lesson handing them money he'd most likely never see again? "Why do you need a car?"

"To get to work," John said.

"You get into too much trouble borrowing money. Better to save and buy something outright."

"Don't worry," John said to Timothy, "I'll ask my folks."

Timothy nodded.

Joshua felt a little guilty refusing someone money when he had it to give, but he wasn't convinced they needed transport to get to work since they lived within walking distance to their place of employment. And he had other plans for the money he'd been saving.

Joshua called for a taxi and when it arrived he took the boys home to their apartment.

John said, "Thanks for coming, Joshua."

"*Jah, denke,* Joshua," Timothy said.

"You're welcome. Keep out of trouble, now, both of you. Okay?"

The two boys nodded before they headed to their apartment building. Then Joshua's thoughts leaped directly back to Adeline. She must be feeling awkward, being there with his younger brothers, Jacob, Samuel, and Benjamin, and his mother and father. He'd have to make it up to her and their Saturday would have to be extra special.

When Joshua arrived home, he saw Adeline sitting in the living room happily talking while everyone listened. She stopped talking when she saw him, a smile lighting her face, and his mother jumped up and hurried over to him.

"What happened?" she asked him.

"Everything's fine. They weren't charged, but their car was destroyed. It wasn't their fault."

"Are you sure they're okay? And how could it not be their fault?"

"Jah, Mamm, they're fine. Some *Englischer* boys were in another car, trying to run John, who was the driver, off the road. Instead the *Englischers* went into the ditch, called the police, and tried to blame John and Timothy. Their plan backfired, though, because there were outstanding warrants against them and the police knew they were troublemakers. So the *Englischers* are in jail, and there are no charges at all against John or Timothy."

"Ah, *gut. Denke,* Joshua. I feel much better. I have your dinner hot in the oven for you. I made, well actually, it was Adeline who made your special onion sauce."

Surprised, he looked over at Adeline. "Really?"

"Adeline why don't you keep Joshua company in the kitchen while he eats his dinner?"

"Okay."

"Don't forget to finish your story when you come back," Samuel said.

"I'll remember." Adeline rose to her feet and headed to the kitchen.

CHAPTER 20

HIS MOTHER GOT his food out of the oven and placed it on the table, and then she left the two of them alone.

"So. I come home, and you're already part of the family."

Adeline giggled. "I've had a really good time. Your family is so nice."

"*Denke.* I think so." He looked down at his food. "Did my *mudder* really allow you to help her in the kitchen?"

"*Jah,* she did. She showed me how you like your onion sauce."

He chuckled. "I can barely believe it. I'll eat this and I'll take you home. We've got a big day tomorrow and it's late already."

"What are we doing?"

"I'm still working out the finer details."

"I'm glad that Timothy didn't get hurt in the accident."

"Me too. I know *Mamm's* worried about him, I am too, but we have to give him over to *Gott.*"

Adeline nodded. "You're right."

"Mm, this is delicious sauce."

Adeline chuckled. "I'm sure it's the same as you've had before."

"It tastes much better now that I know you made it for me."

WHEN JOSHUA FINISHED HIS MEAL, they joined the family in the living room and Adeline told the rest of her story from where it had been interrupted by Joshua's homecoming. Then Adeline said goodnight to his family, and the two of them slipped outside into the fresh night air.

As they walked to the buggy he took hold of her hand. Her hand fit in his as though it belonged. He wanted to share with her how thrilled he was that his mother liked her, but that would make his mother sound like an ogre. He knew Adeline was the one for him, and he'd known it for a long time. She was shy and caring, not bold and brash like some of the other girls he knew. This was the woman he wanted to have children with.

When he reached the buggy, he looked down into

her eyes as she looked up into his. "I don't want to let go of your hand," he whispered.

"Then don't."

A soft chuckle escaped his lips. "I have to for a moment, so I can go around to my side and get into the buggy."

"Just for a moment."

After they both got into the buggy, they joined hands again and neither let go until they reached Adeline's house.

"I can't wait until tomorrow," he said.

"Me too. I'll be waiting."

He gave her hand a small squeeze before he released it. When he saw she was safely inside, he headed back down the darkened driveway to the road.

CATHERINE WAS asleep under a quilt on the couch.

Adeline pulled back the quilt and woke her up, so she could tell her everything that had happened that night. The girls stayed awake most of the night talking.

JOSHUA ARRIVED home to a dark house. Then a light was lit by the couch and he saw his mother and father sitting there, looking half asleep.

"Why aren't you two in bed?" he asked.

"Your *mudder* made me wait up for you."

His mother gently dug his father in the ribs. "Obadiah, you shouldn't say that."

"It's the truth." He chuckled.

He sat down with them. "Are you worried about Timothy?"

"This isn't about Timothy."

"*Nee,* your *mudder* couldn't sleep because she's pleased about the guest you invited for dinner."

"She's a nice girl. Will she be coming here again?" She leaned forward waiting to hear his answer.

"If you must know, we're spending the day together tomorrow."

His mother brought her hands to her chest. "I'm so happy."

"Now can I go to bed, *Mamm?* I've had a busy day."

She leaped to her feet. "*Jah,* go to bed so you're nice and fresh for tomorrow."

"Oh, *Mamm.* Would you care to do something for me?"

"*Jah* of course."

"There's a slight matter of a picnic basket, and the food to go in it. I was going to ask Hazel for help, but the dinner had to be cancelled tonight, so I didn't see her."

"I think I can find some food in the pantry for a picnic."

"*Denke, Mamm.*" With so many men in the house, there was always plenty of food about.

"Now can I go to bed, too?" his father said, grinning from ear-to-ear.

"*Jah.* You didn't have to wait with me."

As Joshua walked up the stairs, he heard his father say to his mother, "You know I can never go to sleep unless you're by my side."

Joshua smiled and he hoped he'd have a marriage like his parents'. They were still very much in love.

CHAPTER 21

THE NEXT MORNING, Joshua was hitching his buggy and excited for his big day when Benjamin, his youngest brother, walked out of the house to join him.

"You know, if you're certain Adeline is right for you—"

"You don't need to give me advice."

"Don't I?"

"*Nee,* you don't. I give you advice," Joshua said.

Benjamin chuckled. "Maybe at work, but not with my relationships."

"I wasn't aware you had a relationship."

"I was just going to say—"

"*Mamm* sent you out here, didn't she?"

Benjamin smiled and looked downward. "She wanted to send Jacob out but he refused. I think he wants Adeline for himself."

"I don't think he does."

"Are you going to marry her?"

"I might."

"Gut. I like her."

"It seems everyone here likes her." Joshua was finished hitching the buggy, and he led the horse away from the barn a few steps. "Goodbye, Benjamin."

Benjamin folded his arms across his chest. "Have a good day. Don't forget to invite me to the wedding."

Joshua chuckled and climbed into the buggy. When he got out onto the road, he trotted the horse, glad that every step was taking him closer to Adeline. It was a perfect day with not a cloud in the sky. Would today be too early to ask her to marry him? Even though he knew she was the woman for him it would only be the first day they spent together.

ADELINE PACED up and down the living room floor waiting for Joshua to collect her. She'd woken early and had dressed in a soft violet-colored dress. Catherine had brushed out her hair and braided it for her while giving her advice for the date. She didn't take much notice of her sister's advice, but listened just the same. Catherine had told her to be sure she didn't agree with everything he said because other girls would've done that. Adeline was going to be herself. Her younger sister had also made sure her cape and apron were just so, and her *kapp* was straight.

When he finally arrived at her house, she said goodbye to her parents who were eating breakfast, and went out to meet him.

"Gude mariye."

"Gude mariye, Joshua." She climbed onto the seat next to him.

He glanced behind him. "I've got a picnic basket packed. My *mudder* helped me with that. It's for later in the day. You've eaten, haven't you?"

"I have. Have you?"

"Jah." As he left her driveway and moved onto the road, he said, "I thought we'd drive to look at some covered bridges and see a few places we wouldn't normally visit."

"I'd love that."

As they drove around looking at beautiful places, Joshua talked about his life and his work in the family business. In turn, she told him about the things that she liked to do. She loved to bake cookies and recently she'd tried her hand at making ice-cream.

"Would you make me some ice-cream?"

"I will. What flavor do you like?"

"As long as it's ice-cream, it doesn't matter. I've liked every flavor I've ever tried."

Adeline giggled. "Me too. I'll make you some soon."

"Wunderbaar, I can't wait." He turned his buggy into a park. "Ready for some lunch?"

"Jah. I'm quite hungry by now. I should've made up the picnic basket. Your *mudder* must think me dreadful."

"Nee. That's not right. I invited you, so it's up to me to bring the food. I cheated, though, and asked *Mamm* to help me. She was only too happy to help." He stopped the buggy, jumped down and pulled out a blanket and a basket.

She climbed down too. "Can I carry something?"

"Nee. You choose where you want us to sit."

"Okay." They walked together for several paces. "What about here, under this beautiful maple?"

"Perfect." He spread out the blanket and they both sat down with the basket between them.

"Let me do the rest."

He chuckled. "All right. I won't argue."

When she opened the basket, she was surprised to see it was filled with dish towels. "What's this?" She picked one up.

"Ach nee! I've picked up the wrong basket. She said it was the one by the door. There were two and ..." He covered his face with his hands. "I don't believe this. I wanted everything to be so perfect."

Adeline laughed. "It doesn't matter."

"Jah, it does. You must think I'm ..." He shook his

head. "I wanted to give you the best day. A day you'd love. And now I've ruined everything by rushing."

"You were rushing?"

He smiled at her. "I couldn't wait to see you this morning."

"I couldn't wait to see you either." She lowered her gaze and knew her cheeks were flushing with color.

"Truly?"

She looked back at him and nodded.

"Adeline, I know you're still young, but when you're old enough would you marry me?"

She stared at him not believing her ears. Even Catherine didn't suggest that he might say that. "Marry?"

"*Jah*, it's a concept where you would become my *fraa* and I'd become your—"

"I didn't expect this."

He drew his eyebrows together. "I'm sorry. It was silly of me to ask. This is only our first real date, but I was just sitting here thinking, wouldn't it be a good story to tell our *kinner*, that I proposed over a picnic basket full of dish towels."

She giggled again at the silliness. "Are you certain?"

"Of course I'm certain, Adeline. I've liked you for a long time. I can't imagine being married to anyone else. I can understand if you want to take things slow because of your age. Even a year or possibly two is okay with me."

"That would be far too long."

"So, does that mean you want to marry me?"

"I do. I'd like to be a young *mudder* and have a large *familye.*"

He chuckled and rubbed his chin. "That suits me just fine. Shall we have twelve *kinner?*"

"I was thinking more like eight. And I like even numbers, so four girls and four boys."

"Perfect."

He LOOKED down at the dish towels, chuckling as he wondered who was eating their picnic, and then looked back at her. "What do you think your parents would say about it?"

"They'll be pleased. They were very happy when Lucy married Levi."

He nodded, remembering that his mother wasn't too happy about Lucy, but Lucy and Levi had been together for a while, so that was a different situation. This was a surprise they were about to spring on everyone.

"Let's go and get some fish and chips. I'm starving. Then, what do you say we stop by the bishop's *haus* and see if we can talk to him about moving forward with our plans?"

"Plans?"

"Marriage plans."

"Before we talk to our parents?"

"Jah. Sometimes people do that."

"Do you mind if we say something to our parents first? I think they'd like to know before the bishop."

"If that's what you'd like to do."

"I would prefer it, please. Is it okay with you if we tell mine first?"

Joshua agreed.

Later, over their meal of fish and chips, they made plans for their future. They'd start by looking for a place to live. Joshua had money saved for a deposit, so they were in a good position to buy a small house.

When they were sitting in front of Adeline's mother and father, with Catherine listening in from the kitchen, Adeline knew her parents wouldn't be able to believe it. Things had happened so fast between herself and Joshua.

"What is it?" Adeline's father asked, frowning at the two of them.

Joshua smiled at Adeline, and then looked back at Mr. Miller. "I've asked Adeline to marry me and she has agreed."

Mr. Miller took a sharp breath and then looked at his wife.

Mrs. Miller raised her eyebrows and stared at Adeline. "Is that right, Adeline?"

She smiled. "It is."

"Are you certain you're not rushing things?" Mr. Miller asked.

"Dat!" Adeline was shocked. Besides that, she didn't want Joshua to start having doubts.

"This is what we both want," Joshua assured him. "This part has happened quickly, but we've both been thinking about it for some time."

Mrs. Miller crossed one leg over the other under her full dress. "What does your *mudder* have to say about this, Joshua?"

Adeline was concerned that her parents didn't seem overjoyed with the news.

"We haven't told them yet," Adeline said. "That's our next stop. I wanted you and *Dat* to be the first to know."

A tiny smile appeared around the corners of Mrs. Miller's mouth. "If you're both sure, then I'm very happy for you."

Instantly, Adeline was relieved. "You are?"

"Of course. We both are," Mr. Miller said. "Why wouldn't we be? You're a fine young woman, and *Gott* has chosen a fine man for you."

Mrs. Fuller bounded to her feet. "Now how about a cup of tea and something to eat? *Nee,* why not stay for dinner, Joshua?"

"Nee denke, Mamm. We have to tell Joshua's parents before their evening meal."

"Oh, where are you both having the evening meal?" her mother asked.

Adeline stared at Joshua, not knowing what to say.

"How about we come back here?" he suggested.

Mrs. Miller nodded, with a grateful smile.

Adeline had never seen such a pleased look on her mother's face. "Would you?"

"Jah, Mrs. Miller, we'll tell my folks and then make our way back here. Is that okay?"

"Wunderbaar," Adeline's mother said, while her father chuckled.

On their way out of the house, Catherine ran out of the kitchen. "Stop!"

Joshua and Adeline both turned around to look at her.

"Don't you have something to tell me?" Catherine asked with brows raised and hands on hips.

Adeline laughed, knowing she'd already heard everything from her listening-spot in the kitchen. "We're getting married."

Catherine squealed and hugged Adeline and then gave Joshua a quick hug. "I can barely believe it. Oh, I'm so excited!"

"We're coming back to eat here as soon as we tell Joshua's parents."

"And … I guess we'll talk to the bishop tomorrow. It'll be too late to do it today," Joshua said.

Adeline wagged a finger at her younger sister. *"Jah,*

so no telling anyone until our wedding date is published."

"I know how to keep a secret." Catherine giggled.

When they were driving to Joshua's house, Adeline held her stomach. "I'm so nervous. Do you think everything will be okay? I mean, will your *mudder* be happy?"

"Jah, she really likes you. I can tell."

"I hope so. I like her too." Adeline sighed. "But she might not like me as a *dochder*-in-law."

"We'll soon find out."

"She's hardly going to tell me if she doesn't like me."

Joshua chuckled. "Just watch her face. She doesn't have to use words to get her point across. Don't worry. She'll be happy, I'm certain of it." He reached out and took hold of her hand.

NOW IT WAS Joshua's turn to be in the hot seat as they sat in front of Mr. and Mrs. Fuller. It was obvious his parents had a pretty good idea what was going on as soon as Joshua had said he and Adeline wanted a word with them in private. Thankfully, none of his brothers had arrived home from wherever they were.

Joshua began, *"Mamm, Dat,* I ..."

Adeline stared at Mrs. Fuller as Mrs. Fuller's eyes opened wide, hanging onto every word her third-eldest son was saying. Mr. Fuller sat with feet wide apart and his hands clasped, twiddling his thumbs in circles. It seemed Mr. Fuller was feeling impatient. He'd been called in from the barn, so Adeline thought he might've been in the middle of a project. Now Joshua was the nervous one, and Adeline was tempted to tell them herself. It would've been a lot quicker.

"So, we're both here today, Adeline and I, because we have something to tell you."

"Well, go on, tell us. We're both ready and waiting." Mrs. Fuller said to her son, and then shot Adeline a grin.

Adeline smiled back, but couldn't help wondering if that smile might be wiped right off Mrs. Fuller's face as soon as she heard the news.

"We're getting married," Joshua said, looking back and forth from mother to father.

Mr. Fuller clapped his hands together once. *"Wunderbaar."*

"Is this true?" Mrs. Fuller asked.

Joshua laughed. *"Jah, Mamm,* it is."

"Then I'm delighted."

"And I'm pleased for both of you, too," said his father.

Adeline put her hand to her heart. She could scarcely believe her ears. Her future mother-in-law approved of her. She hadn't been worried about Mr. Fuller. He'd already seemed to like her the night of Timothy's car-accident woes.

Then Mrs. Fuller jumped up and said to Adeline, "Can I have a hug?"

Adeline stood. "Of course." The two embraced, and then mother and son hugged.

Mr. Fuller shook his son's hand firmly, and gave a nod and a big smile to Adeline.

"We told my parents quickly, before we told you. Now we're going back to have dinner at my parents' house." Adeline held her breath hoping that wouldn't cause friction.

"Of course, it's only right to have dinner there, and Monday night you can both have dinner here. I'll cook up something special. Can you come in the afternoon to help me, Adeline?"

"I'd love to." Adeline remembered Joshua saying his mother didn't like anyone helping her in the kitchen. This invitation meant that Mrs. Fuller truly liked and accepted her. Adeline couldn't have been happier.

JOSHUA STOOD THERE IN HIS PARENTS' living room. He'd been prepared to ignore his mother's wishes regarding his choice in a wife, and now that he knew she liked Adeline, it made everything that much more special. God had found him a wonderful wife and he would work hard to be a good husband—the kind of husband the sweet and shy Adeline deserved.

"*Mamm*, I've been meaning to talk with you about the picnic basket."

"Did you enjoy the food?"

"Tell her about the food, Adeline."

Adeline gave a little giggle. "The dishtowels were tasty."

Mrs. Fuller put both hands up to her cheeks. "*Ach nee!* You took the wrong basket. The one you took is not a picnic basket, Joshua, it's my storage basket."

Adeline kept giggling, Mr. Fuller laughed, so did Joshua and then Mrs. Fuller joined them.

Thank you for reading *Joshua's Choice.*
I hope you are enjoying the series.
If you'd like to receive my new release alerts and special offers, add your email in the 'newsletter' section of my website: www.SamanthaPriceAuthor.com
Blessings,
Samantha Price

SEVEN AMISH BACHELORS

ABOUT SAMANTHA PRICE

USA Today Bestselling author, Samantha Price, wrote stories from a young age, but it wasn't until later in life that she took up writing full time. Formally an artist, she exchanged her paintbrush for the computer and, many best-selling book series later, has never looked back.

Samantha is happiest on her computer lost in the world of her characters. She is best known for the Ettie Smith Amish Mysteries series and the Expectant Amish Widows series.

www.SamanthaPriceAuthor.com

Samantha loves to hear from her readers. Connect with her at:

samantha@samanthapriceauthor.com

www.facebook.com/SamanthaPriceAuthor

Follow Samantha Price on BookBub

Twitter @ AmishRomance

Instagram - SamanthaPriceAuthor

Made in the USA
Las Vegas, NV
12 January 2022